JULES

BY THE SAME AUTHOR

Song-Plays 1983-94
Wormwood (novel) 1997
Nusquama (novel) 2002
Onævia (myth/history) 2003

Cover illustration:

Untitled by Sandra Gevertz (oil on canvas, 203 x 173cm)

WILLIAM DIREEN

JULES

ALPHA BOOKS

ISBN 0-9583266-4-9
©W.Direen 2003

This publication is copyright.
Any unauthorised act with its contents will incur
criminal prosecution or civil claims for damages.
No resemblance to any person living or dead is intended.

You have come in out of the shadow.
You shine with your own light.
You bring your own dark.

W.H.Oliver[1]

Jules opens his window. Sounds erratic yet predictable find him — the wheezing of distant boulevard traffic, the whine of a poorly tuned scooter, the thumping of deliveries to nearby shops. Five floors below, his baker, baker for all tastes and occasions, screws up his nose at the night traces on the pavement. He turns a key that raises his riot blind. Other shopkeepers are already rinsing away the detritus of the lawless hours — dance club flyers, cigarette packets, improvised filters. With each swish, echoes of the night go too, the cries of wrangling street-kids, the rush of fleeting taxis, the sentry-calls of night workers, the irregular steps of stoned club-dancers, and those desperate, repeated taps of half-remembered door codes. Unlike Jules, the local merchants rarely hear these sounds. For them, night is something you sleep through. It is something to be insured against.

Love makes you heedless. When he first came to Paris, he used to amble along rue de Rennes and boulevard Montparnasse at four in the morning. Sometimes, as the black-eyed sky lightened and miraculously healed, Mélita would come to his apartment and they would lie together, toes protruding out the end of his sofa-bed. Born in Algeria, her family shifted to Paris after Algeria gained its independence.[2] She used to sing with a low-paid but sympathetic three-piece band in an ill-lit cavern, scene of Jules' triumph and of his humiliation.

A narrow staircase led to the low-ceilinged club, known as The Cat, short for Catacomb. Ventilation was poor, table lighting by candles, the barmen and waiters cold and sometimes rude. An ancient sewer ran underneath. During the day, without the music or the clatter of glassware, you could hear water flushing, and without the cigar smoke or other odours of the night, a disconcerting mustiness was detectable. A backstage area for staff, as large as the bar itself, ran deeper under the building. From there a rickety wooden stairway led to a security door that opened onto a courtyard.

They met on the days she worked. Jules arrived towards the end of her soundcheck and they dined. If he stayed till she finished singing, they walked home together. He never slept at her place, a tiny former maid's room in the 9th arrondissement.

She chose material made popular by committed singers of the sixties and seventies — Léo Ferré, Georges Brassens, Juliette Greco and Barbara. Jules referred to these artists or their lyrics in the course of his lectures, which made him popular with some students. Finding a person in a painting who resembled Mélita, he took her to see it, but she was disappointed. She had been expecting a Mona Lisa or a clean-lined Venus, not a thumb-sized unfortunate in a Dutch genre painting.[3]

'The model was Jannetge van der Burgh, the painter's wife,' Jules announced proudly.

'The more fool her!' she retorted, and found a portrait for him — the salacious figure of Zeus peeping at a lactating Antiope in the painting by Hendrick Goltzius.[4]

The strain began to tell. Mélita did not want a husband or a family. She had a family, a bitter and abandoned one, and she did not want to find herself mothering Jules. No matter how secure his job or his prospects, his proposition that they live together frightened her and she found ways to keep him at arm's length. She began by telling him that she had other friends, other girlfriends she went to films with, and, eventually, male friends.

It is not unusual to be jealous in Paris, but it is a crime to reveal it. Jules learned that he had much to learn. His childhood model had been a duteous animal-anaesthetiser. His ideal at university had been an over-reaching rock-climber, as inept with women as he was adept with a pickaxe. Jules was ill-prepared for Mélita and fell into her chasm. He was every cliché of the suffering lover — he had tasted of the apple, the arrow was in his heart, he was drunk on the potion, he had it bad.

One of her friends was a young collector called André Vidal. André had not yet developed the tired cynicism of the experienced dealer. He was enthusiastic about the artists he represented, promoted them tirelessly, and was known to take risks on their behalf. He rented a tiny gallery in the Bastille area and was seen at any opening of the slightest interest. It was he who brought Mélita's talent to the attention of an established performer's agent.

After her initial recording success she became an attraction at the Cat, and the dingy nightclub became a cult venue, earning itself such epithets as 'authentic', 'existential', and 'underground Paris'. Being courted by music journalists and members of the art set, Mélita had less time for Jules. One evening, he lay in wait for her outside her apartment. When she left, he followed her to her soundcheck and waited in a nearby café until she had finished. When she took a taxi he took one too, to rue de Lappe and André's gallery. When André and Mélita went to a restaurant, Jules went to the cavern bar and ordered the first of many drinks. He did not notice them arrive together, but when she appeared on stage he assumed André had come with her. When he did not see him at any table, he told himself that he was in the dressing room. Trusting in some quixotic instinct to challenge him to a duel or cut him dead with a well-timed remark, he slipped in there. André was not there and Jules had just removed Mélita's appointments diary from of her bag when she surprised him. There was a scene. Jules was ejected by the musician's exit and told never to return. On his way home he heard a plainchant he had not heard for many years, a lament barely distinguishable from the whisper and purl of night.

> *Where is our lord?*
> *Hidden in the Lady's mirror.*

In all these years he has learned little and ventured less. He has never again wandered along the boulevards in the early morning hours, contributing to the traces erased by shopkeepers at sun-up. In his room he creates his own form of detritus — an ashtray littered with half-burned pipe tobacco, a neglected coffee-lined mug, the crumpled sofa-bed he lay on last night, blinking. There are the things he treasures too — his books, a rare engraving. There is his *Flamma Eterna*, a Pompeian oil lamp, souvenir of a trip to the continent with his father. There is a letter he wrote to Cézanne when he was a boy. It lies in a creased-leather portfolio along with certificates and some documents relating to his parent's house, which he still owns, in Somerset.

Sometimes he hears that they have attended a gallery function or a concert together, André and Mélita. Though they were never 'kidlings blithe and merry',[5] and though their relationship was never as he had imagined it, he avoids occasions when he might meet one or other of them.

He refills the *Flamma Eterna*.

In the night, in the hours of silence, the small flame swells, illuminating all. A naked bronze youth is poised on the cap, hips squared, shoulders turned, looking backwards. His right hand is spread, his left is clenched. As Jules tops up the oil now, figurine in hand, it guts. He lights it again, hand steady. He has passed the point of trembling.

A doctor offered him pills to relax. Always new pills, new guarantees. He tried some sedatives, but instead of fixing the problem of being half-awake all night they made him half-asleep all day. The same doctor advised him to change his habits, experiment a little by joining a gymnasium or a swimming club. He changed doctors. The next one prescribed different sleeping pills, and discovered that his prostate was enlarged. Afraid that they might try to remove it, and recalling that Andy Warhol entered hospital for something routine and came out in a box, Jules abandoned all medicines except cocktails.[6] He would carry his swollen glands about with him. He would brave being unslept, lingering, hungering for what he had never known. Tumescent insomnia would pass away, or he would.

An explosion, like that of a tyre blowing out, causes a flock of sparrows in the plane trees below to take to the air. They dive up and vanish over the lift towers opposite. He clips his brittle toenails. When will they leave off their insidious lengthening? His beard is guilty of this too. He shaves, wiping out forests of masculinity in a single sweep, not without a thought for Polyphemus, the one-eyed monster who mowed his beard with a sickle, sick with love for the nymph Galatea.[7] He draws a suit from a built-in wardrobe. A button is missing from the change pocket but it still holds its form. He lowers a loose Carnaby pullover over the fly and fills the coffee machine thinking, 'Anticalque. Batteries for the laser.' The percolator wakes with a stertorous wheeze and launches a series of sinister gutturals. A mother bawls at her child to get out of bed. A siren on the boulevard blares, strengthens, lowers a quarter-tone and fades. He goes below for bread sharing two floors with the altar boy from Courbet's *Burial at Ornans*.[8]

'Morning, sir.'

'You made it.'

'I came to say goodbye, sir.'

'Where are you off to?'

'You hear that siren? Art cops! They're aiming to wipe us out.'

'You'll be back?'

'Not till they've found other fish to fry.'

'We've known each other a long time. We were the same age then. The incense sent you away from the scene, into my imagination.'

'Not your world, sir. I drift in my world, not yours. It's you who are the invader.'

'Isn't it the same for us all, the gallery of the senses?'

'I don't live in a gallery. You do, your sort! I belong in the real world. That's where I come from! You know what I think? I think you should stick to your own kind, mister!'

The boy vanishes as Jules makes room for a customs

inspector entering at the third floor.

'Bonjour, professor.'

The son of the customs officer attended an open seminar on 'Illusion and Art' conducted by Jules at Port Royal last year. He calls him 'professor' now whenever they meet.

'Over the worst of it.'

'A real summer, that's what we need!'

The lift descends the final floors in silence.

'Did you know the gas is going to be cut off?'

'I saw the notice.'

Although Jules' sleeves are rolled up like someone used to hard physical work, he can do little to dispel the image the customs officer has of him as an eccentric Englishman whom intellectual activity has rendered inattentive. They cross the courtyard, out of step, beneath a three-metre sculpture of Egyptian water bearers. Jules grips an iron handle in his right fist and heaves their great three-framed front portal towards him with all his murder-latent strength.

'Doesn't get any lighter.'

'That's very good of you, professor.'

They both know its weight. The former owner of the building could not open it a crack. He lived on the top floor and used to call the caretaker before leaving his apartment.

The customs inspector waves down his bus just in time. It will connect him to the metro and a regional train, the RER. Ninety minutes later he will pass through a security screen at Roissy Airport. Jules crosses to the bakery rotating his arm, wincing at a twinge in the cartilage of his right shoulder. He quickens his pace to keep clear of a cleaning truck jetting water left and right. Dollops and ephemera skip into the gutters on the other side of the street sending up odours of atomised dung and traces of phenol. Jules joins a three-member queue. Let's strike up his theme tune now. Something fast and repetitive, like early Michael Nyman, or a techno sample with baroque strings dropping in unannounced. The baker is standing behind the counter as if he has been expecting not any chance crust-cruncher but this one in particular. He winks at Jules and reaches for two croissants, his regular order now for some weeks. The baker's movements, fluid and practised, ride the music, whose hundreds of staccato beats create a single impression like the rapids of a mountain river.

'Et un bâtard, s'il vous plait.'

He smiles at Jules' English accent as more bread-buyers join the line behind him. Inspired by the theme music, they break into a Hallelujah! and are just dividing into barbershop harmonies when Jules takes the croissants and the stick of bread and turns. Silence. A computer repairman is searching his pockets for the right change. A part-time child-minder is gazing inconsolably at a chocolate Easter egg decorated with a frill of cerulean and pink icing.

On the footpath a massive, heavily-clad man with tusks of hair radiating from his nostrils asks Jules for 'just one franc.' Jules gives him the few cents change from the bread, because the word *franc* has reminded him of the twentieth century, of his boyhood, and, by association, of England. Traffic has stopped at the lights. As he crosses the glistening street, he glances up towards two open windows — his own, and that of the cellist on the floor below him.

He puts his shoulder into the door and ascends alone, chewing the crusty knob at the end of the *bâtard*, reading automatically: 'IF A BUTTON DOES NOT WORK PRESS IT AGAIN TO DISABLE COMMAND THEN TRY AGAIN. IN CASE OF DOORS NOT OPENING PRESS BUTTON 'A' AND ANSWER THE QUESTIONS OF THE VOICE.'

What would the face behind the voice be like? What would the voice ask? Would he know the answers?

The lift was installed when the former proprietor grew too infirm to take the stairs. Despite the urging of relatives, he would not budge from the top floor. Two adults fit uncomfortably within.

'Good morning.'

'Bonjour.'

Then the Frenchman, 'Bye bye.'

And the Englishman, 'Yes! Goodbye, monsieur.'

He has never had reason to press a button twice. He has never pressed button 'A'. That voice, would it be human?

The coffee-machine has spat its reserve and is gurgling out the last few drops when he returns to the apartment. The sun has found his window. Though weakened by the outer plaque and double panes, it fills the room sufficiently to annihilate the flame of his oil lamp. Is it indeed still burning? He reaches his palm towards the wick till he feels the bite of the flame.

'Alive, at least.'

Along the boulevards thousands of cars are sleeking, streaming to the centre, to their underground parking spaces, exhaling 'Paris' with the force of a great return. There are the usual hold-ups. Some of the drivers curse traffic jams, some curse motorways. Few consider that they *are* the traffic jams, that they define the motorways. At the airports around Paris there are the usual queues and delays, security is tight. An incoming passenger from London is preparing his part in a guessing game he and Jules play when they meet. This time Owens has discovered a curious fact relating to haircuts in the Middle Ages. He is surprised that Jules has held down his job in Paris with the kind of haircut he goes for.

They met in 1984 in the British Museum, where Owens was researching the moral satires of Hogarth.[9] Heading for a degree from Britain's only Institute of Criminology, Owens was a man who paid particular attention to his appearance. His suit was firm-fitting, excellently-tailored and his manners were genteel, though he soon revealed an underlying want of self-control. He and Jules were near-opposites, and it was a type of compensation for each that they should become friends.

An identikit picture had been published in the Times that morning, a police department reconstruction of the face of an unidentified victim of the King's Cross Underground fire.

'Look at that! The bareness, the... the barrenness... the emptiness of that face. What does it say to you?'

'Nothing. Why should it? It lacks personality.'

'Exactly. Fleshed-out bone structure. Or a living face without muscles, without personality. Imagine, it might be a head of a cadaver injected with Formalin. They are preserved so as not to putrefy, but the musculature is inactive.

You've attended autopsies?'

'One. I vomited.'

'You know something else? It's what Lombroso would have called a criminaloid face.[10] We've been studying him, his types of face — the born criminal, the insane criminal and the criminaloid. The born criminal has a large jaw and cheekbones; big ears, or very small ones, eye defects and pouches in the cheek, like those in some animals—'

'What year are we in?'

'The 1870s.'

'Weren't the Nazis interested in that?'

'All scientists were. Later they shifted focus to body types — tall and sinewy, muscled, short and fleshy, that sort of thing. A German, Kretschmer, identified each body type with a specific crime.'

'Before the war or after it?'

'Before and after it. He studied thousands of cases.'

'So what category do you fit into?'[11]

'Ectomorphic, 'pyknic' type, prone to manic depressive disorders!'

'And me? Go ahead, I'm thick skinned.'

'Don't you think we should have a proper drink?'

It was the first of many drinking sessions and conversations on similar themes. Jules never did find out his own physiognomic category. If he had pressed Owens to tell him, he would have learned he was an 'asthenic' type with polytropic criminal potential.

Jules was accepted for his post in Paris, and just before he moved to France, in a split-level coffeehouse near Oxford Street, Owens announced he was going places as well — to Texas, where he was going to witness an execution.

'Wouldn't you, Wells? If you could have gone to see a witch burn at the stake, or a thief having his neck broken, you would have, wouldn't you, in the Middle Ages?'

'I don't think so.'

'Why not?'

'I am not interested. Art has nothing to do with witnessing executions.'

'Even the Virgin Mary went to see Jesus hang, didn't she? Isn't that in all the paintings?'

'He was her own flesh and blood!'

'But seriously, man! To see the end of hope! The finiteness of the path!'

'Diderot believed the populace would save every criminal it went to see executed, if it could. I'm with him.'[12]

'No, Wells. The populace is hungry for death. They are fascinated by the power of the state to kill. Don't you see?

It's like murdering your own child. It's like executing the powerless, illiterate child, one the state refuses to acknowledge as its own. To be present at that will be the completion of my research.'

'To witness a poor sod wriggling on the end of a hook?'

'To witness Draco's punishment... the written code of Athens revisited. The X-factor connecting the first with the last and most powerful democracy of all time!'

Owens got to carry out an interview and witness the execution. The condemned man had never been afraid of anything in his life, and he said he was not afraid of death itself, but he did not want to die in pain. He had heard that the person who gives the injections sometimes mixes up the four different chemicals in their tubes and he was afraid that the poison, which has a very painful action, might be administered ahead of the anaesthetic. In order to have the wherewithal to cry out, he was the first condemned man to refuse tranquillisers on the morning of the event since the recent escalation in executions.

Two years later, Owens' researches made numerous visits to France necessary and he has been a regular visitor ever since. Their conversations range from physiognomy to the genetic sciences, from serial killers to megalomania. Jules has never tired of Owens' company. Immersed in late-medieval art and researching such things as popular prophecies pertaining to the Apocalypse, Jules has a tendency to become monastic in his habits. Owens throws open the windows of his cell. Some say that without friendship and the spontaneity that goes with it, personality itself ceases to exist. When Jules is with Owens, he feels resuscitated.

The furze of morning unravels. Jules takes a folder marked 'Design of I' from his bookshelves. It is faded along the spine, its sticker is peeling and pages are spilling out on three sides. He cups his hand round the base, tenderly, as one of Botticelli's ideal virgins supports the backside of the Christ child.[13] He places the folder on his desk and leafs through the text of his lecture. The latest changes are in architect dark purple. Every year he adds or deletes, coding the changes with coloured pens. He returns to the shelves to check out some statistics, taking a book from head height. He blows its topmost edge, sending a jet of dust fanfaring into the sunlight. He has not taken this book more recently than... than when? Since he sat for his portrait, when he passed the time memorising quotes. It was the only way he could keep his mind off the person painting him. He opens

The Plague in Holland.[14] In fact, it opened itself. He has read this page of figures before, many times before. The spines of his books have a memory of their own.

He notes the statistic he was looking for on the back of a used envelope. A phrase occurs to him with which to conclude the lecture: 'Ignorant, corrupted, guilty, all that remained was to be sentenced.' He repeats it aloud and jots that down as well, stuffing the envelope in his vest pocket. He is about to close *The Plague in Holland* when he notices a groove, such as one a metal point stylus might make, leading to a crater. A second trail deepens to a gouge that penetrates some of his glosses. It is mirrored on the opposite page, on consecutive pages, and there are dots of excrement not in the channels but towards the gutter. They roll, dry as century seed. The printed text has largely been spared. Thoughtful little weevil. It might still be there, in the spine, or has it emigrated to sample more of his library? And how did it get into his demesne? The student who did his portrait... she borrowed it for a few days... could she have given it to him? If so, textually transmitted, like the revenge of the Brazilian spider...

It was his first holiday from university study. He was at home helping his father clear some papers out of the attic

— decades-old documents relating to alterations and repairs, the property's plumbing, district council permits and the electricity wiring. His father passed them down through the trapdoor. Some were in rolls, others in folders. Many had similar channels in them.

They were drinking English Breakfast Tea at four in the afternoon when he felt a burning in his armpit. He scratched, it worsened. He ran to the bathroom and threw off his shirt. A shiny black abdomen with a white dotted cross fell into the tub. A moment later, as shocked as Jules was, it spread slender ladylike legs and vainly tried to ascend the slippery enamel.

'You!' Jules screamed, as if he recognized the spider.

His father came running. Mrs Wells too. She gave him arnica tablets and smeared cream over the bites, identifiable by a red blush round white nodes of irritation. Mr Wells sealed the spider in a jar and examined it saying, 'Poor little octopede. Man fears spider no more than spider fears man.' The cream was beginning to bubble, Jules' skin was goose-pimpling, the rash was spreading fourteenth century vermilion. He felt a terrible tiredness in his arm, his left hand. Soon it was all he could do to bend his fingers. And as he did so, the burning sensation became intolerable, and the ends of his fingers froze as if about to strike. His fingers had become exactly like the legs of that spider, bending tentatively, gynaecologically, at the tips. They rushed to the village.

The doctor dabbled with paint in his spare time and he was also something of a classicist. He welcomed the chance to treat Mr Wells' famous student of art history. He lanced the bites at the points of penetration, and gave Jules a pink ointment for the wound.

'Look at the sheen of that cream! There's chemistry for you! You know, Hippocrates wasn't only the father of medicine, he was the mother of all pigment. *Pharmaka* and *pharmakeia* translate not only as 'medicines' but also as 'colours', you know?'

'Really? Oh, yes.'

'Not forgetting Pliny.'[15]

'You've got me there.'

'*Medicamen*, for dyes, especially rouge, an artificial means of improving a natural product. Book Thirty Five, if I'm not mistaken. Poisons, drugs, other colouring matter.'

'Gosh! Yes, of course.'

'And Virgil.'

'No! Really?'

'*Venenum,* poison, medicine, paint. Corroboration found in Horace and Ovid.'

'And I'm supposed to be the art expert!'

'*Fucati medicamenta ruboris et candoris.*'

Jules looked blank.

'Counterfeiting dyes of dazzling white and red. Cicero.'

'Ah, yes. So few paintings from his epoch have survived. We'll be doing the ancients next semester.'

'Yes, you will be! You've been given a reprieve. You might have copped it, you know. A rare species. Brazilian.'

The sun has passed like a kindly laser from Cranach to Dürer, the vertical shadows of the window frames are plumb with the spines of his compulsively arranged books. The titles of his 'bilingual' texts are clearly illuminated.

Shamed by the doctor, his next acquisitions were Virgil, Hippocrates and Pliny. From the last he learned that Nero commissioned a colossal painting of himself which was struck by lightning. This sparked an interest in the *hubris*, the vanity of commissioning, which led to the patronage of Philip le Bon, one of his specialist subjects. It also led him to a swift swivelling dancer — his first silverfish. Poor hungry fugitive. No wonder Pliny asked of some such creature, 'At what point on its surface did Nature place sight? Where did she attach taste? What does it feel? What senses does it have?' None, not after Jules had brought his fist down on the flyleaf. It metamorphosed instantly into dust.

There are those he will never see, search as he might. That one, for instance — he darts a quick glance at *The Plague in Holland*, hoping to catch the culprit or its descendant peeping from one of the thoroughfares of its incessant breakfasting. Out jumps nothing. There is a time when it is better to fumigate. There are experts....

Jules is saved from the complete insectification of his thoughts by music — deep, unhurried notes, rich with the beauty of their instrument. A rosined bow has arched across four receptive strings. The cello responds like a cat that likes to be stroked. He has been waiting for it.

It began just two months ago when, during an unseasonably warm spell, he left a window open all night and heard her warming up at breakfast time. By leaning precariously out his own window, he ascertained that the sounds were coming from the open window directly below his. He came to recognize the piece she was practising, and, on successive mornings he was disappointed if he didn't hear it. By now he had been exchanging polite hellos with the new tenant in the building, a cellist with the Ensemble Intercontemporain. Brief conversations followed, going to or returning from the bakery, about renovations on the block or a change to the door code, in which he discovered her first name was Norma. Then, two weeks ago, they found themselves on the same bus heading towards Palais Royal.

Jules was on his way to an auction of medieval artefacts at Richelieu-Drouot so they looked at the catalogue together. He was especially interested in a fragment from an illuminated manuscript, which had been discovered in the cellar of a building once attached to a monastery near Metz. Norma noticed that all of the senses were represented in some way or other, a lute for hearing, food on oval plates for taste, open windows for the sense of smell.[16]

'That's a strange looking dog. It wouldn't be a pig, would it?'

'It might be. What about sight?'

'Those learned types, perhaps.'

'Won't you come and have a look at it with me? It's a world of its own at Drouot, full of craziness and surprises.'

Norma knew of the auctions rooms as dusty halls where drab dilettantes crane their necks over musty boxes. 'I'd love to professor, but I don't have time. *Daphnis and Chloë* is looming, and I have to buy strings for my cello.' She was, it is true, on her way to rue de Rome, where stringed-instrument shops abound. 'Do you play any instrument yourself?'

'I took music lessons when I was child, but my teacher

used to tap my knuckles with a ruler!'

'No wonder you didn't make any progress!'

'And what about you? Do you draw?'

'Only on the music staff.'

'There are pages of notation on offer!' He leafed energetically through the catalogue to a reproduction of a 13th century hymn for two voices. Norma was interested in the fifth musical cell of the notation. It appeared to contain a *torculus,* or *ternaria*, which represented a kind of ornamentation.[17]

'I didn't know ornamentation like that existed in the thirteenth century.'

'Won't you come and look at that, then?'

'Sorry professor. I've made an appointment.'

Jules wished her all the best with the Ravel score and descended the stop before Opéra. It had been warm in the bus and his blood was racing, his own body heat was rising from under his open-necked shirt. A chilly breeze on boulevard des Italiens caused him to button up his padded rainjacket. A few spots of rain bore out that morning's forecast of a dank late-winter's day. It seemed to Jules that everybody on the wide pavements was hastening their step, and he was almost running when he reached the auction rooms.

He registered with the officials and leaned over the

miniature with a magnifying glass, examining the interlacing acanthus of its border with the air of an expert. The vendor had anticipated the question of authorship. To the left of the fragment was a reproduction of an undamaged original of 'Roman Customs'. There was a table of revellers, and at the table three sets of lovers in various stages of courtship (ranging from the courtly introduction to the horizontal conclusion). He now saw that the fragment on sale was missing a second table situated above the strange animal which Norma had thought was a pig. At this table was a man in the throes of a vomiting spell. Other revellers recoiled in disgust. He was glad Norma had not seen that. On the other hand, he was greatly taken with the beauty of the page of medieval plainchant in which she had identified some possible grace notes. The square forms of the signs for single notes, so-called neumes, were intensely black against creamy, durable vellum. The neumes were like flags, now square, now lozenge-shaped. Where they were connected to make up melismata — in which one syllable is sung over the course of several notes — they looked like the formidable, stone steps of medieval castles. One of the overseers told him it provided a rare example of temporal note-value dating from before 1200. The reserve price, he added, was quite low for its market value.

Jules was taken with an urge to make a grand gesture, to bid for the music notation, to outbid his rivals, to pay the price and to offer the page to Norma. Not understanding the process, bidding was well underway before he raised his hand. The reserve price had already been passed and so had the balance in his bank account. Luckily for him, an unseen purchaser entered the fray, and, using a coded signal understood only by the auctioneers, secured the object of Jules' desire for himself.

He left the auction rooms five hours after he had entered them in very poor spirits. Cloud continued to lower over the city. A sprinkling of icy drops was anointing the ever-hurrying late-February shoppers. As he returned to rue de l'Opéra the skies opened. He waited in the doorway of a closed bank facing the neo-baroque Palais Garnier, in whose hidden vaults Gaston Leroux's disfigured Phantom of the Opera held his victim captive. There was something irresistibly hearty about Norma. She did not have the air of a victim. She did not appear to have walked out of an advertisement, but he would happily have bought any product she was recommending. She did not look like a film star, but he would have gone to see every one of her films. As he rode home he was sure that this, at last, was love.

The upholsterer has arrived in his workshop over the canyon. Sometimes the sounds of hammering or of his compression air gun reach Jules above the calamities of the street. On calm summer days the derivative he uses for gluing intoxicates half the neighbourhood. He is standing at his window in a cowhide leather apron, sleeves rolled up like quoits, exposing his tattooed triceps and ulnars. Jules takes off his glasses and faces his neighbour square-on, inhaling, hoping he won't make any pneumatic noises just yet. The men hold their positions, without giving each other the slightest signal. Norma begins practice-proper:

> *Daphnis, his love carried off by pirates, is sleeping.*
> *The sun rises and birds begin to sing.*[18]

Divorced from the other parts of the orchestra, and from other cellos, a piece results whose tied semi-breves and dotted minims are a call to courtship, note for portentous note. He has been doing his utmost to meet her again, in the lift, in the bakery, by the letterboxes. She is the reason for his early-morning excursions to the bakery.

SECTION 172.
Chloë sees the young nymph wandering on the meadow.

Before his shaving mirror he lays on the *medicamen* and the *venenum*. All scents compatible, brows incontestable, clean contacts in position, blinking easily, dust-free, holding. Now for the plumbing. The music does not reach in there.

'A confused prostate, Monsieur Wells.' The doctor had a hand on each of Jules' knees, having removed the glove of prognostication. 'Only human in midlife, a bit of a swelling here and there.'

Jules asked for a note for his doctor in England and offered to pay the final account immediately. He was not going to England, but he was going to change doctors immediately.

Reluctantly, tenderly, he closes the windows on Norma's performance. In reverence, he nibbles a few flakes from the end of a croissant before setting it back on the table. He takes the winding stairs to ground level, descending like a counterweight for the lift, which is rising up the spigot of the spiral stairs, occupant or occupants unseen.

In a retro sixties suit endowed by wear with a hint of Iraqi sands, he passes the Librairie Vocabulaire and a little bar, Le Provençal, where he sometimes shouts his models a drink after he has drawn them. There is his pharmacy, and the doorway of his optician framed by imposing sheets of red marble. The bank is already doing good business, its automatic doors open and close in perfect silence.

Jules does not have time to waste, but he does not appear to be in a hurry, not in the Parisian way. He is somewhat unpolished, in their view. Laborious, unspectacular, but a convincing self-portrait in employable dimensions. His lines are fluid, like soapy water, and his suits, after all, are well-tailored, evoking the epoch and nature of his origins. Easily sized up, here is a man who shouldn't let you down.

A tall figure and a diminutive one approach, a governess holding the hand of her immaculate charge who, in the morning light, seems to be shining like the little girl in Rembrandt's *The Night Watch*. Or is it that Jules contacts are not properly seated? The girl passes asking, 'Why does the Queen want to cut off their heads?' as Jules is rolling his eyeballs around like a horror-film ghoul. He dabs at tears that have already reached his nostrils, thinking, inevitably, of Saint Lucy. In painting she is the saint most associated with vision. Her eyes were put out by a tormentor and miraculously restored. Diocletian commanded that she be defiled in a brothel, but the Lord firmed up her portals. In paintings the eyeballs used to be depicted loose, in a dish.

Orbs in their sockets, contacts seated, Jules eases past the remaining pedestrians. The locals have less the look of Lucy about them since a squat near the station was cleaned out. Political refugees, asylum seekers, drug addicts and runaways no longer add colour to the neighbourhood. Police raided the pre-war tenement one chilly dawn and took its occupants away for a good drubbing and identification. The building was bricked up, the roof removed, and a demolition order now promises that its future will be brief. Not for very much longer will its smashed upper-floor windows wave those fragments of sooty lace.

Alert to the psychopathy of morning traffic, giving no indication of his unslept state, Jules crosses peppily to the

RER entrance. If you were watching him, even through a coarse security camera, you would never guess that a button is missing from the change pocket of his trousers. You would not suspect that he sees figures invisible to everyone else. There! A virgin. Not just any virgin. The first one. Thick wavy fair hair. Apple-faced. A pulpy roundness suggesting idle cupidity. It is the Eve of Lucas van Leyden, *his* Eve, the Eve of the print on his wall at home, an authentic sixteenth-century engraving he found at the St Ouen flea markets.

He had gone with a visiting Argentinean researcher into that maze of thematic warehouses hoping that she would be enchanted by the fantastic collections and find him equally wonderful, but she struck up a conversation in a tiny café where some of her compatriots were strumming cattle songs and Jules went on alone, of a mind to take a gamble. A print with a moralistic theme caught his eye. It had been softened by mould and nibbled by weevils. It was the frame that was for sale, not really the print, but underneath it he identified some closely-set parallel lines known as hatching, which could only have been the shading of a second work. Whether the second work would be an improvement on the first was anybody's guess.

Back in his apartment he peeled away the eighteenth century engraving of a moustachioed gentleman listening complacently to his angelic daughter's lute playing and, millimetre by millimetre, a gift from heaven was revealed.

The work proved to be faulted at the time of execution but was well preserved, measuring the correct eight centimetres by twelve, depicting the Original Sin and dated 1529.[20] It is a print from Lucas's final years when he believed fellow artists had poisoned him. It might be the very engraving referred to by Vasari as 'the command of God not to eat the apple', or the next in a series. The snake is particularly penile. An apple is stuffed in its mouth. It is not placing the apple directly into Eve's hand as in Dürer's earlier work, the she-devil is not offering Eve a second apple, as in Willem Vrelant's version, nor does Adam have two apples as in another engraving. Here Eve already has one apple, the first apple, while the one in the devil's mouth suggests a limitless supply.[21] Adam and Eve are like brother and sister, their feet are almost identical in position, in shape, even in the spacing of the toes. Brother and sister? Or father and daughter? In this engraving, it is impossible to forget that Eve is, in a sense, Adam's daughter, nor that they are destined for hard labour, for pain in childbirth and for agony in dying.

As for the curvilinear hatching that caught Jules' eye, it was the bark of a tree. Other hatching lines radiate from the rim of a hill representing a battle between light and dark which light, on the horizon, is losing — this because of the majority of shade over white. So Jules supposed it was a sunset and not a sunrise, or if a dawn, the dawn of the end of paradise. The characteristic L is there too, where it should be, singing the L of Lucas and of Leyden, doubly denying the artist's father's name of Jacobsz. A previous owner had probably concealed it during the Second World War, or an earlier war, and died with his secret. It was flawed in that the ink was uneven, so it had survived Lucas's own rigorous incineration of faulted prints. It had survived concealment, war, incineration and insanity and it was his, as if by fatal design, for a cattle song.

Eve is standing near an air vent, tresses floating. That is Paris for you. You can be the naked incarnation of the mother of humankind and no one pays you any heed. He would like to draw her there, but there isn't time.

At home, that is the place to draw subjects. He rings them in. It is paid work, and not so very different from their usual occupation. Grosz uglified them. Rouault divined their auras. Dégas gave them texture. Picasso limned them. And Jules? What does he do to his naked and poorly-remunerated women? The caretaker of his apartment block is wondering just the same thing. Eve takes a bite of her apple. Jules looks at the station clock. Stopped.

A breeze scoots along the platform with its scent of the overground. The RER has been stringing the bead-stations since before sunrise, skating the dawn-light, wheeling and braking, closing and opening doors, warning and jamming — Charles de Gaulle, Gare du Nord, Orly-Sud, now overland, now threading the wormhole. The driver sights a metal flag at the end of the platform. He is punctual to the minute of the clock of the control brain, if not that of the station. The brute muzzle eels in, bearing, braking, halting in 200 metres, the gliding behemoth is hindered, nose to the node of maximum penetration. The doors of the fourth car are before the feet of Jules. Eve finds a seat further down the carriage. She crosses her legs elegantly. Jules detects a suggestion of printer's ink. Doors wedge the world out. The driver stokes the electro-worm. His consignment feels the pull, the train surges to maximum speed and cruises through space, through opacity. They are winding and descending by a sort of mental peristalsis through the continuum, guided by a raw sense of masked light and of gravity.

The passengers are brought to a gentle halt. Eve has vanished. A host of petulant schoolgirls is passing beneath the egg-shaped model of a liposuction advertisement just as Adam appears, disoriented but of noble stride, abdominally and shoulder-strong, divinely buttocked. Noble, if eternally lost. The mythical rib-donor pauses before a wall-map of the metro circuit. Should Jules offer to help him? Could he avert the Fall? No, it must be too late, and he would miss his connection. He leaves the world of the RER, of steady gradation, of cushioned vibrations, and enters that of its diminutive relative, one of rattling carriages and synchronised jiggling: the metro.

On the platform a little boy wearing Mickey Mouse ears asks his mother when the Disney train will arrive.

'You'll feel the wind, honey.'

She has a Brooklyn accent that helps her to display all of her affection for her child while disguising none of her boredom with motherhood.

'Who'll be driving the train, mom?'

'Merlin, honey.'

'How does he make it move?'

'With his magic baton, honey.'

The boy and his mother make it inside the carriage before anyone else. Commuters exchange diffident glances, or stare at liposuction ads, or into space — space as yet remains at this hour in the gelatine throng. It is a pasteuriser's nightmare. Cleaning women, tramps and diplomats shove against each other. 'Attention please. Pickpockets are known to be active on this train!' People check their pockets, their bags, their neighbours. Sweat competes with perfume. The metabolic squeeze becomes too much for some, who stare numbly through the windows into the darkness outside. In the curved glass, they sometimes become aware of their own reflections, elongated or distorted in unexpected ways.

The doors open at last and the Brooklyn mother has discovered this is not the train for Disneyland. She pushes her way out, dragging her infant behind her. The operation of giving and taking room repeats. Scents and codes are again exchanged. It is a time of day, if not a section of line, where there is a correct way of behaving — you ignore your opposite, you give room and you are given room, anything approaching courtliness is out of place. Sometimes there is a chance meeting.

In a city with an outer population rising to fifteen million you wouldn't expect to meet anyone you knew, but it often happens. If you follow a furrow between nest, interchange and work station, it only takes a slight variation of timetable or routine to cross someone you know. When recognition occurs, exchanges are high pitched, hurried summaries of lives. You catch up, you scribble a number, you promise to call. No excuse is needed to escape, since neither of you has any time.

A boy has entered the carriage — St John, the youngest of the disciples in a fresco by Tommaso di Giovanni di Simone Guidi, otherwise known as Masaccio.[22] In the painting St John is to the left of St Peter. The figure of John is believed to be a self-portrait of the artist himself. Masaccio died at 27 so suddenly that many suspected he had been poisoned. His name translates roughly as Shabby Tom. The man who carried the impetus of western painting from Giotto to Michelangelo was, conceivably, murdered as a consequence of his sloppy dress habits. In a half-convincing Russian accent, the boy announces that he is an asylum seeker from Kyrgizstan, where he was persecuted by a sect linked to the Taliban. He is waiting for a decision on his status as a political refugee. He appeals to the passengers for a few coins, a restaurant ticket, or a cigarette, working his way through the carriage with his hand held out. Not one of the commuters responds. It is as if he does not exist for them, and even though his hand is appealing to them, he himself is not. It is as if they do not exist for him.

The morning is not a good time, thinks Jules. In the morning people are preparing for the day to come. He would have more luck when people are tired, but when they have a sense of completion. That is when they might be more generous.

A commuter near Jules clenches his fist, and hooks his other hand around a vertical pole. His contorted body is contradicted by an impassive, pasty face. He clenches his fist even more tightly, as if within it is proof, or a voice, or the secret that prevents him from falling. Jules takes the envelope from his pocket and repeats the phrase to himself: 'All that remained was to be sentenced.'

The boy reaches the end of the carriage and wishes everyone Good Day. He and Jules and a few others descend as a figure in a khaki jacket races from the platform up the exit steps. There is always someone late for an appointment in the city, though not usually someone in surplus military clothing. As the warning tones of the doors sound, a woman shouts from inside the carriage, 'My bag! He stole my bag!' The doors are forced open by two hefty sporting types who leap from the carriage onto the boy. They pin him to the concrete, and beat him with their fists. Jules enters the fray, pushing the smaller of them off balance and yelling at the other that they have made a mistake. The men step back, as much because of the staining power of the blood they have caused to flow as Jules' entreaties. Seeing that Jules is respectably dressed, they mutter something about the police before moving off down the platform rubbing their knuckles. Jules gives his handkerchief to the boy who suppresses a sob, swears at the woman who accused him, insults the men by calling their mothers whores, and finally ridicules Jules himself, who is already heading up the exits steps, unaware that his envelope has slipped from his pocket. A woman seated on the top step is holding out her hand. Her leg has been severed at the knee. A unicorn, four-legged and proud-horned, is featured on a billboard advertising the Cluny museum. The text reads *Mon Seul Désir*.

As he takes a quiet lane to the Arts School, a grimacing beggar leaps out of a lane entrance and cavorts around him, pivoting on his crutches and jingling his ankle bells. His tongue is lolling, his nostrils widened, and he is fixing Jules inquisitively, accusingly. He has escaped from a work by Bruegel, called *The Beggars*.[24] His feet do not touch the ground at all as he spins on one crutch and swings the other one around like a sword, nearly decapitating Jules in the process. An envoy from an another century of misery and madness, he sings:

I may be ugly I may be poor
But I earned my wounds in the holy war
Defending our dirt for the likes of you
Who cling on for life to your filthy sous.
What do you know of the people's feud?
I never seen such decrepitude!
Do you belong to the human race?
You should be lumping a carapace!
With nothing but needing and no means to pay
Our children learn early down penury's way
Though our water is foul though we've scraps in the bowl
Though we sleep with each other like rats in a hole
You are the one with the head full of stuffing!
You are the one with a heart full of nothing!

Jules turns the palms of his hands upwards as if to say, 'What can I do about your predicament?' A police siren is heard not far away. The beggar cries out, 'The Duke of Alba!' and returns to the recesses of Jules' mind.

The gesture Jules has just made might have been that of a well-slept man wondering whether he felt a drop of rain. Many of the gestures of the disappearing resemble the gestures of the sane. And so he repeats the gesture looking at the sky. He shakes his head, and continues on his way to the college, turning down a familiar lane that leads towards the gates of his faculty. No matter where he descends from the metro or which route he then takes, he always arrives at this final leg of the journey. Each day, after turning this corner, he looks to the end of the lane towards a sculpture above the gates — a copy of a Roman emulation of a Greek *Eros Aloft*. As he does so he unconsciously establishes the degree of humidity, temperature, and atmospheric pressure 'that define [this] day from all others',[25] before glancing into the window of an African and Pacific art boutique. The display has changed. Today there is a sculpture from Nigeria in the window, a woman smoking a sort of pipe. She has spiral scarification on her cheeks, in form not unlike the tattoos of the Maori, while heavy beads terminating in bells cross between her firm breasts in the manner of gaucho bulletstraps.

Now he is whistling joylessly to himself. It is not a sound that would be audible to a passer-by, but more of a whisper caused by the passage of air over his teeth, his lips, and his tongue. The sonic confusion of street and underground have exiled *Daphnis and Chloë* from his memory. Any melody might arise now, even the most banal. It is a student-review tune. Every year the same melody accompanied different lyrics. The tune had been handed down for generations and was played on a pre-war upright piano in the concert hall of their residential college. Jules' room-mate Teddy Moore wrote the words one year and premiered his version with a quartet of fellow rugby players dressed like Soho whores. Thereafter, it was hollered whenever revellers reached the required level of intoxication.

Teddy Moore would probably have conquered Mount Everest had he lived. He was highly popular and never lacked company. Jules was no champion physically and was alone much of the time. Yet when Jules was obliged to consider sharing a room in his second year, it was Teddy, who had no money worries, who suggested they would make good flatmates.

Noble, knightly Teddy Moore was on a climbing expedition in Tanzania when he fell a few metres onto hard rock. He put ice on the bruise, laughed it off and roped himself to the mountain correctly. He hadn't broken any bones and insisted to his fellow climbers that he was fine, but a cyst in his abdomen had burst open and infection was spreading quickly. It would have been a simple enough matter to fly him out if he had admitted that all was not right, but he took his nausea and dizziness to be a consequence of the altitude and he pushed himself ever harder to keep up with the rest of the team before falling again. This time the ropes caught him. This time he didn't laugh it off. His temperature shot up. The vomiting started. It was already too late.

Jules was one of the pall bearers. At the ceremony and afterwards he met people Teddy had talked about. It seemed they had not known him at all. He had known him. And during the following months he returned. No footsteps crossing the boards of the college museum were anonymous, they belonged to him. He haunted the very stone of their residential college. His face appeared in the windows of the King's Cross Chapel. His phrases, his manner of dealing with situations recurred in Jules' phrases, in his manner. He possessed him like a breathing force. When the symptoms were still mild, Jules told himself, much as Teddy had told himself on the mountain face, that nothing was amiss, but eventually he had to admit that this death had disturbed him at a fantastic depth.

The psycho-analyst alluded to the grief of widows for their husbands, and the traumas brought about by sudden splits in relationships. He suggested that what Jules had felt for Teddy was an emotion such as might exist between family members, between close friends or *between lovers*. Jules was aware that when he was close to women, to certain women, he felt sexually aroused, but he had never considered that there had been a homo-erotic element in their relationship. There had never been any clearly-definable sexual moment between them, but, as he paid the psychoanalyst off, he admitted that such a moment might also be eternally hidden, that this was the love Jules could feel for a man.

In Manchester, Leeds and in London, where he held fellowships and junior teaching positions, he formed dependable professional attachments, the kind he has with Marcel in Paris. They never intruded on his private life, but the cast of his private life was thinning. He was nearing the end of his time in London and applying for permanent positions all around the world when his father fell ill. In Somerset, before retiring one night, he examined his face in the mirror and identified his father's and his mother's faces. An eyebrow arched as his father's did, a fold of skin was developing into a flap such as one on his mother's face. He identified Teddy Moore in his own face and was not surprised. He had simply adopted one or other of his muscular responses which had affected his malleable features. Finally, and this did upset him, he recognized himself. It was a younger self, separated from him by no more than the speed of light, but it was enough for him to feel divided, to feel that his perception of himself was that of a stranger.

He immersed himself in his researches, rebuffing potential sexual partners. All his aspirations became intellectual. When he gained the position in Paris he believed he would now be fulfilled. Filled mainly with self-importance, he lost his former self-control. In the city that appeared to have adopted him, well-salaried, respected, flattered a little, he fell irredeemably in love with a woman he was incapable of loving.

'Good morning, sir!'

The words issue from a small mounted weatherproof speaker. Jules responds with a grim nod of the head towards the guardian of the gates. A voice behind him cries vigorously, 'Professor Wells!'

'Miss... Radich?'

'Radstock. I went to the Daguerreotype exhibition. 'I'm so glad you recommended it.'

She feels they have something in common because they are from the same mining country. She monopolised him at the grand opening of Le Plateau. She spilled her drink over his shoes at the BANG launch, Palais de Tokyo.[26]

'Oh, yes. You enjoyed it, then?'

His hand goes into his jacket pocket where his fingers

inadvertently open the silver wrapping of a crushed-nut Belgian chocolate.

'Wonderful. I'll mention it in my essay, but not if you don't think it's relevant.'

'It's not that. It's just ... be careful, you know, of easy comparisons between works belonging to different genres.'

'Yes, but, well. That's what I wanted to say. I'd really like to discuss it with you. I... could we talk about it later, if you have time?'

His fingers are covered in chocolate and soft centre. He can't possibly remove his hand to look at his diary now. 'Friday is good for me. Tell Madam Torres I said so.'

'Oh good... yes... fine... thanks.'

As she leaves him and passes out the gates he wonders how it is young women find it in themselves to walk at all. It must be an inexpressible pleasure. He finds a forgotten handkerchief in his rear pocket, wipes the chocolate from his fingers and discards it in a nearby bin. As he steps up onto the stone slabs of the Vitruvian cloister a figure approaches, now fiercely lit, now darkened. Will it be real?

'Professor Wells? Good morning.'

'Good ... Good morning.'

'I... I came by yesterday. You... weren't in your office.'

She is German, and sporting rectangular spectacles.

Sonja Kaufmann. A thin, triangular face. She installs squares of complementary opposites, under black or strobing lights. He avoids her because she reminds him of a certain Italian panel. That's not her fault, of course, but there is a little Jules inside him, an impressionable Jules, who could fall hopelessly under the spell of a Lorenzetti virgin.[27] Sometimes paintings hit him like that. When he first saw that work, he had digested the justifications of experts who now attributed it to Lorenzetti but he was suffering more acutely than ever from a feeling that often creeps up on him when he is in the Louvre — an embarrassment, a discomfort at his own presumptuousness. That face among so much Byzantine metalwork penetrated him to the core.

'Make another appointment, could you? I'm sorry, I have a lecture this morning.'

'Yes, of course. I know you do. I'm on my way there. I'm flat out as well! This afternoon, then?'

She is wearing a tightly-buttoned shin-length suede coat, dainty boots and a bright clementine scarf.

'Should be... yes, pretty certain.'

Guilty. She knows already he will not be there.

He leaves the public domain of the corridor and enters Madame Torres' office.

'Did the student from Berlin find you?'

'Yes.'

'Yes, good. What a day!'

'Lovely! Spring is sprung!'

She hands him his mail. 'You haven't heard?'

'Heard what?'

'There was a riot at Nation. My son was arrested.'

'I am sorry. Is he all right?'

'In shock.'

She is poorly slept, but determined to be efficient. 'Mister Owens called.'

'From London?'

'He's in town.'

'Did he say where he's staying?'

'He said he'd ring back.'

He gains his office and opens a letter telling him he has been granted a budget for a new series of lectures. He could shout with joy! He disables the smoke detector, opens a window, and lights a hand-carved, whalebone pipe. His thoughts turn to the lecture. He runs through the main points. He searches for the envelope and failing to find it, he tries to remember the statistics he noted down. How many times was the city of Leyden struck by the plague? And what about that ending? It was a triple construction, 'Ignorant, flawed, corrupted' wasn't it? It doesn't have the same ring as it had this morning. 'Corrupted, ignorant, flawed.' That doesn't sound any better. 'It only remained to be —', what was the last word? 'Sentenced' does not feel right. He tells himself not to panic, it will come back to him when the adrenalin is charging.

He takes a mirror and a pair of rapier-thin scissors from his desk drawer, props the mirror up and snips some loose hair-ends. He keeps his appearance theatrically conventional if not criminally exact. He has aged as his teenage idols have, preserving that counter-grade, post–avant-garde look. There. Two or three locks carefully displaced and you have the controlled wild of one who survived the age of Pop.

He renews the batteries in his laser pointer and tests the red pinlight on the palm of his hand, following the deepest lines as if with the tip of a scalpel. A boy on the street recently shone a pointer in his eyes. He was shocked but not wounded. There are commercial saboteurs who specialise in lasers. One hit in the eye and a rival, a greyhound or a champion horse, staggers on its pins. And, of course, there is laser surgery. He fears that more than having his prostate cut out.

The optometrist's lights were red, the main one, and a green one out to the right. When he could no longer distinguish between the C and the O, she applied some drops and his eye closed involuntarily. Anaesthetised, his pupil dilated, a steel instrument peeled back the outer edges of each lid. She searched his darkness, opening and closing spectral bands of light, widening and narrowing shutters, examining. The bands resembled now gates, now the interstices of a code. The lenses of the machine retracted as she framed, surveyed him, desensitised, demobilised. Her own iris flexing alert, she invaginated him. He counted the seconds till his liberation, understanding how enslaved sight might be worse than blindness, how it was that Democritus, so the story goes, put out his eyes rather than suffer reduced hours of contemplation. That blackness, so sheer, without any spatial quality; the sudden light of his examiner, piercing, freezing onto him; the fear that his retina was growing an irreparable heather, that the day would come when no information would stick — it all revived his distrust of doctors.

'A failed operation is rare, Mr Wells.'

'I'll wait to see if there is any improvement.'

'The chances of failure are one in ten thousand, and patient vision improves a hundred times for every one who shows no improvement. All they do is lift off the corneal flap and make the adjustments. You can see on the same day.'

'How much is that in francs?'

Owens once sent Jules a postcard from London of St George poking out the eye of a dragon. The eye of a storm, perhaps that of God, is in a direct line with St George's lance.[28] Jules pinned the postcard on the notice board of the staff-room; he took it down when the optometrist frightened him with talk of surgery.

He follows the corridor to the third door right, hands Yassim, the technician, a note with details of last-minute changes and, with a brisk stride, enters the hubbub of the lecture theatre. Here is a man of indeterminate years, refreshed after a good night's sleep, ready for business. How can they know he has not slept for days and is being sought by gang of dispossessed pall-bearers? The rustling in the auditorium dies down.

'In an edict published at Worms in 1497, the Emperor Maximilian declared that the French pox was a punishment for blasphemy.' Yassim brings up a slide of a woodcut showing the infant Jesus, seated in the lap of the Virgin Mary, sending arrows of disease upon two repentant sinners.[29] A corpse lies in the foreground. 'In 1499, Corradino Gilino wrote, "Our Supreme Creator, full of wrath with us for our terrible sins, punishes us with the cruellest of ills which has now spread across almost the whole of Christendom."'[30] The next slides appear more or less on cue, but before long an image is at odds with the text. It is Jules' fault, his pages have become muddled and he has arrived prematurely at Gerrit Dou.

'His technique stems directly from his teacher Rembrandt's early work, which we looked at last time.' He hesitates a moment, having realised his mistake. 'Dou was renowned for his delicacy of detail. Almost blind at thirty, his near-obsessive miniaturist realism can be read as a reverse symptom of his condition. We know that he was an obsessive cleaner. "...[O]ne remarks that he ground his colours on a mirror, that he took infinite precautions to prevent their being *corrupted* by a single speck of dust, that he always cleaned his palette himself and even the handles of his brushes." So the Comte de Caylus. Could you bring up the slide titled, *The Physician*, please Yassim?'[31]

A blinding square results, accompanied by groans from the students then, amazingly, the correct slide appears. Jules' laser pointer dashes metres across the screen. 'The woman's suspense is evident. The doctor is reading the urine flask like a clairvoyant reading a crystal ball. *The Young Mother*, please.'[32]

'You can hardly see the doctor in this one, but there he is in a darkened rear room reading his urine flask again, like a shadow in the mind of the young woman. The attention of the baby has been drawn by the rattle of a little girl, a common enough moment. But is this distraction not a clue? Both adults and children are prone to be distracted by glitter and meaningless noises. Note the detail here, the shimmer of the candlestick, the grain of the floorboards, the tassels on the chair, the fur trimming of the mother's jacket. Is this attention to superficial reality more than a display of virtuosity? *Pearl Necklace* please.[33] The woman is possibly pregnant. A lover is referred to in three ways: this heavy cloak, this note on the table, and these two chairs whose positioning draws us into the frame. There are symbols of vanity here — the powder brush — and of pride — the mirror. The joy of the young woman is near-spiritual, so pure that we are almost won over by it. But notice the sinister counter-weights, the voluminous dark urn and the carelessly deposited cloak. It is a carefully counterpoised work, and an ambiguous one. The pearl itself was known as a symbol both of virginity and of vanity. Ermine fur symbolised both chastity and pretension. According to legend, the ermine, a kind of weasel, would die if its pure white coat were soiled. It is a painting full of premonition, of foreboding, which avoids any sort of preaching. *The Sick Woman* please![34] This one speaks for itself. Metsu's patient can't so much as lift her gaze towards her weeping carer, nor raise a bloodless hand to make the slightest gesture. Beside her enervated limbs the sharp detail of her fur trim appears frivolous, earthly. Here everything is too late. Here death will be the only victor. Now for a painting you must all be familiar with by now.'

Gerrit Dou's *Dropsical Woman* appears.[35]

'The subject has swooned away as the doctor was making

his diagnosis. His hand shows his unease. Note the indices of dissolution, and the next chance you get, see the way the light in the painting seems to fail before your eyes. Dou's painstaking work can be read as an appeal for spiritual light, as well as a cry for absolution. Dropsy was regarded as a shameful disease until quite recently. Incidentally, my compatriot Edward Gibbon suffered from it in the nineteenth century. He was so ashamed that he concealed it from his nearest and dearest.'

One or two students show some interest. One or two think he is talking about a monkey. A gibbon at Vincennes zoo is undergoing chemotherapy for cancer.

'Now, to return to the fifteenth century, Dou's *predecessor, Lucas van Leyden* —', Jules gives the words special weight as a signal to Yassim, '— suffered from a mental illness. Tortured by the delusion that he had been poisoned, during the last years of his life he worked mostly in bed. Many of his figures at this time are remarkably virile, muscular, above all healthy bodies, though his own health, both physical and mental, was deteriorating. The slide *Farmhand and the Milkmaid*, please.'[36]

No slide appears. There are some clicks from the technician's box. In the half-darkness Yassim throw his hands in the air. Jules returns to his notes but can't find his place. He is angry at the feebleness of his desk lamp, but more angry with own failing eyesight. He can no longer read the addenda he scratched in when his eyesight was 20/20. He asks for the house lights to be brought up and refers students to a reproduction in their recommended text. There is an autumnal shuffle as some turn to the page while others shift along a place or two to look at a neighbour's copy.

'Take a look at that farmhand and this milkmaid, how they are of a kind with the cattle. Their feet have been strengthened by labour. Beasts and humans are locked into a relationship of hardship, a cycle of nutrition, survival and reproduction, while he who engraved them was wasting away.'

As they inspect the reproduction he has a chance to quickly scan the students. They are the usual mixture of tendencies and styles, invented, borrowed, or purchased. He passes over their faces until he comes upon one who is staring brazenly at him. She is occupying a flip-down seat at the end of a row half-way down the aisle. She is wearing a densely-woven military-style jacket. Medium-length, uncombed hair is trailing over the collar. She does not show any interest in the relationship between illness and art. Jules makes the slightest of signs of complicity and calls for the next slide.

'Do you have *Woman with a Doe*, Yassim?'[37]

Yassim's hand emerges from the technician's box with its thumb raised in affirmation. The house lights lower and an image of a particularly stocky woman, a barbaric huntress, fearfully similar to the woman he has just communicated with, is projected at forty times its real size.

> *I eat the hearts of the mild*
> *I break their necks*
> *I am the namer, the tamer*
> *I am the savage, Diana.*

'Lucas's Diana is robust, earthy, capable of controlling the animals in her domain, capable of killing them. Her body is, you might say, hunting-honed.'

When he thought it up seven years ago Jules was proud of that expression, 'hunting-honed'. Now it sounds artificial. He puts a line through the words and looks up. The flip-down seat at the end of the row is empty. His own Woman with a Doe has vanished.

'When we consider the artist's health, both physical and mental, it is impossible to look at this next work, *The Toothache*, without being aware of certain preoccupations.[38] As the sufferer is being operated on, fingers are slipping into his money pouch. As he submits to surgery, hoping to be relieved of his pain, he is relieved of his earnings. Lucas van Leyden's daughter wrote that the artist destroyed faulty prints by fire. He was most particular about this. He did not want a single imperfect print to survive. He had the right, you might say, and yet this action, is it not like the medical one of cauterising, of searing tissue rendered abnormal by an affliction? His daughter, incidentally, delivered a healthy son 9 days before the delirious master died in 1533.'

The lecture now follows its correct course through the sixteenth and into the seventeenth century. He points to the inherent melancholy of much Dutch genre painting as a sign of intense collective grief before turning to the indomitable energy and humour of later artists, Franz van Mieris the Elder and Jan Steen, to the turbulent energy of a Rubens mythological scene, and to the cheerful endeavour of Gabriel Metsu. He presents these as a kind of resistance to the horror of the last of the plague years. The psychological examinations of the self by Leyden's most famous son, Rembrandt, are held up as a virtual remedy.

To conclude, he returns to some of the subjects they have covered during the series. He mentions the role of free will in the theology of predestination which accounts for the title of the series, *The Design of Illness*. He outlines the reigning fears of the epoch, of natural disasters, of the apocalypse, of divine retribution for sin. He finishes with the painters he began with.[39] His pointer picks out some weevils, owls and winged devils in works by Bosch. He translates curious expressions of the time, the Old German, *vule slecke,* 'dirty slug', not forgetting *een hovaerdich slecken* 'arrogant little slimy slug', which causes a ripple of laughter to pass through the auditorium.

'Amusing as they might be, popular insults reveal the preoccupations of the society from which they are drawn. Creepy crawlies inhabited the imagination as revenging agents of the divine. Soundness of body was equated with spiritual well-being. Safe conduct was the consequence of wisdom — Bruegel's *Proverbs*, please! Accident was the consequence of folly. Folly, like bad behaviour, was tantamount to sin. The mishaps, maladies and mad episodes which we, today, ascribe to bad luck or poor planning, were the issue and evidence of human imperfection, unalterable attribute of a brief existence. Plague struck the city of Leyden on thirty-four separate occasions between 1469 and 1666. Metsu's Amsterdam was hit thirty-seven times. Hooch's Rotterdam, thirty times. Goltzius' Haarlem, seventeen times. Vermeer's Delft, sixteen times, if I'm not mistaken.

Life expectancy at the time was thirty five years. In 1530, when his town was in the grip of an epidemic known as the English Sweat, the Burgomaster of Leyden wrote, 'There is great poverty and terrible hunger. The wretched people are suffering all the time and every day someone says, *O dear God, give us quick release, for we would rather die than go on living.*' It was as good a response as any, on your way to an early grave, to shave your head as Job did, and offer your life back to the Creator. Foolish, flawed, afflicted, all that remained was to be judged.'[40]

The last slide is an altar panel by Petrus Christus in which the spread-legged skeletal figure of Death appears to be giving birth to... the eternally damned.

The house lights strengthen and some of the students have questions. One takes issue with the fact that Jules always refers to the artist in the masculine. Jules assures her it is a linguistic not a mental construct. Another finds the way Eve is depicted in primitive art humiliating to women. He refers her to certain critics and promises to discuss this later in the year. A third asks why personages in paintings with religious themes are never depicted making love. A collective titter ensues, peppered with a groan or two. He ventures a reply:

'Let's say... let's say it's caused by something other than

prudery! Let's say there are different... different kinds of touch, and that each carries a meaning precisely because the... the sexual act... is not described. There's Adam and Eve hand in hand, biting into the same apple... there's Eve rising out of Adam's body... and in representations of Christ — who came to redeem mankind for its sin — there is the kiss of Judas... there is Thomas putting his fingers into the wound of Christ... there is the woman who anoints Jesus while he is alive... and there is the interdiction to touch him when Mary Magdalene sees him as a gardener — an interdiction that makes the terra cotta by Domenico of Paris so poignant.[41] Mary Magdalene is embracing the right arm of the crucified Christ, he who went voluntarily to his death, he who was ready to die. The crucifixion is a psycho-sexual transgression, a kind of auto-mutilation of the celibate martyr-prince. Death becomes a highly charged and exclusive enfolding. *Noli me tangere!* Do not touch me unless it is to prove that I am real, that my wounds are true. But not for pleasure. *For I am death.*'

The students are liberated. The auditorium clears. Some head directly for the bus or train, some chat idly in the corridors, in the medieval cloister, in the garden square. A few, very few, discuss the lecture.

Jules congratulates Yassim, who hands Jules the cassette

recording of the lecture for his archive. In the department Madam Torres is holding out an envelope for him.

'A student handed it in.'

'A mature one, a bit on the rough side?'

She looks up at Jules over the rims of her glasses. She thinks she knows him better than his own mother. 'Yes, professor. She is perhaps with the military?' One of Madam Torres' eyes has a floating blood-patch in the corner. Her son's bad behaviour will be the death of her. Marcel is in the mail room.

'Fan mail?'

'No, no. I must have dropped it in the corridor.'

'These riots... were there many missing from your lecture?'

'Full house.'

'Everything all right, Jules? You seem a bit nervous!'

'I went over time. Watch batteries.'

'Winter runs them down. What was it?'

'The Design of Illness — last instalment.'

'Ah! The pathology of microscopic attention to detail. I remember it! Are you going tonight?'

'Where to?'

'Vidal's new gallery on the quay.'

'I didn't know.'

'I didn't either until just now. His invitations always come at the last minute'

'Owens is in town. You remember him?'

'How could I forget him?'

'Would you like to join us?'

'Thanks, but I'm spoken for.'

'Marcel, you... you wouldn't have a cigarette, would you?'

'Now you're becoming really French! Keep the packet!'

A friendship without rivalry. Jules guided Marcel towards a better understanding of some American critics, and Marcel helped Jules garnish his lectures with popular French expressions. Jules is dark, moody, alcoholic. Marcel is brilliant, charming, ambitious.

In his office Jules puts the cassette recording of his class into a fake-walnut stained bookcase with brass corner brackets whose tacks are popping out. It is an appropriately dilapidated receptacle for the record of his years as an academic: lectures and broadcasts, debates and expostulations on themes as diverse as pilgrimage, Pelagianism and pornography.

He goes to his desk and finds the invitation from André Vidal. He puts his feet up and takes a cigarette, taps it and slips it between his lips. Practised, cinematic, the action dates him quite as much as the library of cassettes does. He has a view of the building opposite. Reflections off his window prevent the librarian in the binding department from seeing what he is up to. Of course she sees the smoke.

The day has changed character again. It looks like rain. He takes the returned envelope and lifts from it a thin slip of paper, a page from a waiter's notebook. On it a crossroads has been awkwardly sketched. A few signs indicate a church, a park, a bookshop and a café, with initials for the names of the streets. There is no other note and no rendezvous hour.

He stubs out the cigarette on the rim of his metal waste paper basket, forever empty for that purpose, and flicks the butt out the window. He grabs the phone.

'Madame Torres. Mr Owens...'

'Yes, Professor?'

'When he calls back, tell him apéritifs, Au Chat Gris, would you?'

'Yes, all right.' She is disappointed. She views Owens as a threat to her efficiency.

He takes a raincoat, a light brown diplomat's Burberry, from a hook behind his door, slips it around his shoulders and goes through the mail room to the corridor. He passes into and out of pools of bold, golden sunlight while whistling that student melody again. A cleaner watches him go, shaking his head.

At the metro station, he passes through retracted pneumatic-powered panels to the boarding platform. The student Sonya boards after him and descends hastily at Maubert-Mutualité where the breakneck voyaging from station to station is suspended for longer than usual. The doors of the train to the deserted platform remain open. The driver announces that due to a passenger falling on the lines at Bastille, the train must remain where it is for another few minutes. He thanks his passengers for their patience and understanding. Some schoolchildren at the other end of the carriage raise a raucous, impatient clatter. As the heat and humidity increase, Jules decides to finish his journey on foot. He climbs towards the sound of traffic, towards the aroma of roasting chestnuts, towards the outlines of Linden leaves blurred by unprotecting daylight.

When he first came to Paris he lost his way nearly every day. Call it Parisian trickery. One of Franz Kafka's characters was aware that the streets 'branch unexpectedly at any moment and at all angles',[42] and Edgar Allen Poe was no less intrigued by the Paris streets. The frontages of the buildings rarely give an accurate indication of the volume they are concealing. Many facades announcing large, spacious buildings, are fronts for wedge-shaped fire-traps housing meagre rooms that not even absurd wealth can render comfortable. 45° corners are common, 30° or 15° not unheard of. Unlike those in the village he grew up in, where a few wide streets intersect at 90° and sight-lines are linear as laser beams, here any suggestion of Cartesian rectitude is illusory. The streets and alleys and facades are surface units in a revolving volume whose values alter like the balls in a gambling drum which are themselves turning. You might pinpoint your position, but once you have taken a few steps, and if you are not familiar with the terrain, that perception of reality no longer applies, the perspectives and volumes have transmuted. The most likely outcome of trying to find your way in Paris is to lose it.

It was through being regularly disauthenticated that Jules stopped exploring the city for its edifices and sculptures and was content with a walk around the block. Just to walk a mile and end up where he began became a source of low-order bliss. 1000 paces. *Mille passus*. The geographical or nautical mile, standardised at 6080 British feet, the value of the geoid at latitude 48° North, is a one minute turn of the great globe, earth. The word mile, like the word *franc*, reminds him of another century, of other places. It makes him homesick for London and nostalgic for Rome. Its use, or rather its retention, and that of a thousand other Latinisms common to English, reminds him of that fundamental fallacy promulgated by his teachers, that Britain was founded by the Romans.

He has arrived at a bookshop whose owner is an expert on Roman history. Bob, a Canadian, devotes most of his free time to translating the epigrams of Martial. Since the eighties he has managed to make ends meet by supplying academic texts from the English-speaking world. He hasn't yet placed Jules' orders.

'I thought of you this morning. There's a new translation of Apuleius's *Metamorphoses* from Oxford.'[43]

'I'll have a look at it when it arrives.'

Bob clears his throat, purses his lips and rubs his lower lip. He is not usually at a loss for words. Jules ventures a remark about Apuleius, 'He was into the black arts wasn't he?'

'Accused of it. He retired from public life to write.'

Again the conversation falters. Bob cannot bring himself to look at Jules, who begins to browse the shelves. Bob snips open a bundle of paperbacks and asks in an offhand way, 'Have you been following the news? Recessions everywhere.'

'Yes. Tough times ahead for all.'

'The fact is, regarding your books. I've written a memo to myself. Here we are, *Iconography of the Miraculous* and, what was the other one... *Genetic Imaging*. T.B.C. To be confirmed. I suppose it was something about funding, was it? To be honest with you, I'm going through a bad patch and —'

'You can order them. I got approval this morning. *Iconography of the Miraculous* will be on the reading list.'

'Excellent! Shall we say... how many?'

'Twenty for the moment. I'll tell them they can get it from you.'

'And *Metamorphoses?*'

'Yes please! Order it. One copy just for me.'

Bob's eyes are on the screen. He says 'OK' again and again in response to prompts. His right hand manipulates the mouse, 'By the way, my consignment of *Pop Weasels* has flawed copies.' He rummages under his desk with his left hand and, without taking his eyes off the screen, brings out the English translation, recently published in London, of Marcel's highly popular book on Pop Art. Some pages are unreadable. A second text has somehow been transferred in negative onto the positive print.

'They must have been stacked before the ink had dried... or else the ink itself wasn't properly concocted!'

'He'll be disappointed. How many copies are like that?'

'Isn't one enough? He should contact his publisher.'

'He's bringing out another one.'

'Oh yes? What about?'

'Art which sells even though the artist is anti-capitalist.'

'What's he going to call it?'

'At this stage, he's thinking of *Fill My Moneybag*.'

'That's a fruitcake title.'

'All titles are fruitcake, aren't they?'

'That would be a better title!'

'You suggest one then.'

'Sure! How about... *Brand Anti-Brand?* Just a minute. Print! There! It's working again!' A noise like the one Jules' electric train-set used to make comes from under the counter.

Bob releases his grip on the mouse, 'Yeah, titles! That's what's important these days. Titles and covers! The book has to sell itself! I should be ashamed of myself! I've become a unit in the global book business. I used to get sample copies, you know, and I could recommend titles. My opinion used to count for something. Not any more. Now I have to log in to read extracts on privileged sites. I used to write letters, they took longer to complete and send and it took time for the replies to come in, but I was dealing with someone... someone real. Now it's the passive tense: *Your request has been passed on. You will be notified.* It's an industry running on automatic. It has managed to eliminate thought. The best-produced books are the ones with the smallest distribution, university texts for salaried types like you who can afford them. And you know what's the final irony? It's ruining my eyesight. How many writers went blind working by candlelight? I'm going blind staring at pixels generated by programmers who know the price of books but not their value, as Wilde put it! And for what? I don't communicate with anyone who will admit to being a real person... that would make them responsible. I hardly have time to read any real literature. I stare at a light-generated text masquerading as the printed word. An impression of an impression on a page. The publishers control criticism more than ever before. They control the web sites, that's for sure. Readers are buying anything. *Anything at all!*'

'I've heard that publishers will soon be selling their texts on-line and readers will print and bind them themselves. Don't you think that might develop a sense of the medium?'

'Fat chance. First up, it's more than just having a medium for the message. It's a matter of having an agent for the transfer of the medium. Even if it's possible to craft books at home, they'll tire of the monotony of printing and binding and opt for the download. They'll compile indiscriminately and never read. Downloadable literature, that has to be hogwash! Hogwash that will kill my business!'

'Doesn't the internet have any advantages at all?'

'None at all. I'm hoping like hell it gets eclipsed by another fad. And you know, last week, thanks to the internet, I heard from a guy I thought had died.'

'Good news!'

'Bad news! Thanks to the net he is about to do just that

— die! He's sick and he's going to set up cameras so everyone can see him snuff it.'

'He's going to do it himself?'

'It looks that way. He says he doesn't want to dissolve in a hospital bed. He wants to go out fighting!'

'He's not mad then!'

'I guess not. I should tell him my troubles.'

'They can't be that bad!'

'Worse! I sell more comic books than novels! Students feel they are getting something special when they get hold of classy comic art in their burger-greased fingers. And some of them are better than any novel I've read for ten years.'

'Really?'

'Sure! Here's one for you. Didn't you write your Ph.D. on Hogarth?'

'Not me. You're thinking of Owens, the criminologist. He's a Hogarth man.'

'Take a look anyway.'

' I'm seeing him tonight. Do you want to come along?'

'I go home nights. There's someone there who loves me.'

Jules realises he doesn't know the first thing about Bob. The colourised cover of the large-format, hard-covered, solidly-bound comic book has a cartoon-character's body in place of the cadaver of Hogarth's engraving, *The Reward of Cruelty*. The intestines of the cartoon-character, Bleako, are being fed into a slops bucket as in the original. So too, his heart has been fed to a dog, and his cranium is being lifted aloft by means of a pulley and an eye-holed hook screwed into his skull. Twenty or so learned gentlemen wearing mortar board hats and wigs watch the dissection with no more than academic interest. On the inside of the front cover we are advised to read the comic book while listening to *Music is Rotted One Note* by Squarepusher at *maximum permissible volume*...[44]

Bleako at the Eye Doctor

Bleako has short legs and arms and a tubby trunk. His head is disproportionately large for his body and his eyes are disproportionately large for his face. They bulge. His hair is cropped on top but long at the sides. It darts out horizontally above his ears making him look like a frightened clown. He is already known to readers. This is one more in a series of titles such as *Bleako Burns Down the Supermarket*, and *Bleako Busts the Cops*. In the first frames he visits an eye specialist called Doctor Birdmann. The Doctor has a long sharp nose, a small pointed mouth, small eyes and shrunken-looking ears on a perfectly symmetrical face. He is bald except for a cluster of tufts of different lengths protruding from the top of his crown. These curve backwards like the feathers of a cockatoo. He holds up a card. Bleako's eyesight is good, exceptionally good, but Aaghh! the pain gnawing at his insides! Doctor Birdmann makes a cursory inspection and discovers that Bleako's knee joints are swollen, his back is crooked and his reactions are slow. But none of this accounts for the pain.

Now there is a frame with Bleako gasping for joy. The pain has gone, the spots have disappeared, he can walk straight, his health is restored but, Aargh! he is blind! His pupils are no more than pin-pricks in their irises. Doctor Birdmann recoils. Bleako is wandering around the consulting room like a ghoul, a zombie!

Doctor Birdmann is perplexed but he likes a good puzzle. He creates a forum: Why is Bleako in so much pain when he can see, and why does the pain disappear when he is blind? Specialists put in their oars. They publish their results. *The Dark Way to Better Health* becomes a best seller. Thinking types adopt him as the symbol of contemporary man. *The Self-Enfeebling Eye* is translated into eight languages. Doctors offer to blind him surgically and poets urge him to degenerate for all he is worth. Bleako doesn't want either. Is there not some middle way?

That gives Dr Birdmann an idea. He announces he is going to take out one of Bleako's eyes. This causes a violent debate among the scientists and thinking types. The scientists are against it because they didn't think of it. The thinking types pooh-pooh the idea as going off half-cocked.

Doctor Birdmann raises a talon in the air (for when he takes off his white coat he is indeed part-bird and part-man, he has huge folded wings whose elbows rise above his shoulders in a beautiful jack-knife). He winks and asks Bleako there and then, 'Left eye or right?'

This sobers Bleako up. He hasn't asked himself that all-important question. He pales, he breaks out in a sweat. What if he puts out the wrong one? Is one eye not logical and the other imaginative? Does one eye not see objects in themselves, and the other objects in their surroundings? How can he possibly choose?

The demonic doctor looks at his watch and taps his toenails. Something resembling pity enters his expression and he makes an exceptional offer: death or blindness with a no-lose clause. 'If you don't like being dead you can try the blindness option and vice versa!'

Bleako chooses death.

When he is dead, he and the doctor fly around for a while, and behold if Bleako doesn't start to feel queasy again, just as he did when he was alive. The good doctor puts his wing around him. He had been afraid of that. It was not vision making him ill, it was what he saw.

Bleako doesn't want to be brought back to life — blindness would not remove this knowledge — but he asks that he be sent to some other world where what he sees will make him feel better.

The doctor is sorry, but the only options are Hell and Heaven, the one full of honestly bad people and the other full of hypocritical goodies. There is one last possibility — lobotomy.

The last frame shows the hemispheres of a brain bisected by a dripping meat cleaver.

Δ

The shaded buildings on Quai Montebello have a leaden pallor, a few trees on Île de la Cité are reflecting off widow-peaked swells whose tips in the mud-honey flow are tinged crimson from an indefinable source as Jules' inhabited Burberry approaches Pont au Double. It pauses at an embankment bookstall and hovers over a 17th century edition of Augustine's *Confessions*.[45] The parchment of the cover, originally part of a 14th century document handwritten in Latin, was recycled in 1609. Augustine speaks somewhere of opening the Bible at random and finding everything was clear. Jules opens Augustine and reads the following passage:

I was too proud to call myself a child. I was inflated with self-esteem, which made me think myself a great man.

In the margin are the words 'Paul, Corinth. XIII, x–xii', written by hand using an ink darker than the print. He tries another section at random.

...we had been both school fellows and playmates. But he was not then my friend, nor indeed ever became my friend, in the true sense of the term... A few days after, during my absence, the fever returned and he died. My heart was utterly darkened by this sorrow.

Without hesitation, he writes a cheque for the book and takes it to a seat by the river. He rarely denies the impulse. 'You never regret having bought a book,' his father said when they were in London for the day, and Jules now has hundreds, perhaps thousands of books, though few as rare as this one. As he crosses to the benches a business launch draws near, driving upstream at full steam, at the prow a group of bankers balancing champagne glasses. If it weren't for their manifest puissance, you would find them utterly ridiculous. With the river before him and Notre Dame at his back, he reopens the book at Book Four, chapter four and reads:

My heart was utterly darkened by this sorrow and everywhere I looked I saw death. My native place was a torture room to me and my father's house a strange unhappiness. And all the things I had done with him — now that he was gone — became a frightful torment. My eyes sought him everywhere, but they did not see him; and I hated all places because he was not in them, because they could not say to me, "Look, he is coming," as they did when he was alive and absent. I became a hard riddle to myself, and I asked my soul why she was so downcast and why this disquieted me so, but she did not know how to answer me.

'You never regret having bought a book. You only ever regret not having bought one.'

It was 1956, a summer holiday. He was eight years old. His mother was up at five to accompany them to the station. In the morning dark they passed the gnarled arms of a village oak which would one day topple through the church's stained glass windows. He was alone in the back seat. The horizon was turning light blue — day as a kind of dilution. Inside the station electric lights were spinning diaphanous, concentric, yellow-gold cocoons around their bulbs. His mother seemed suddenly small and irresistibly weak on the platform. He wanted to stay with her, to drive back with her in the cumbersome Wolseley, to help her to clean the foul house, to forget London existed. But beads of moisture were gathering on the window key, it slipped in his hand when he tried to turn it and she was sliding sideways away from him. Soon the train was rollicking disrespectfully through the waking countryside. They passed the thin parallel lines of freshly furrowed paddocks. He remembers the untimely smell of alcohol from his father's travel flask and he remembers the cold. A dial for regulating the temperature was pointing at a red thermometer, but an Arctic current of air was chilling them from a vent above the window. When his father asked him if he was warm enough he lied. The metal surfaces lost their gleam and the conductor appeared. He knew Mr Wells. They chatted for a while about blood-sucking northern fowl mites which had returned with the warmer weather. Some egg-handlers had developed dermatitis, hens were losing weight and cocks were suffering reduced sperm counts.

They approached London, passing isolated grocer shops

and suburban cinemas, rows of terraced houses without gardens, and tiny garden plots without houses. The connection between buildings and inhabitants became unclear. There were constructions with uncertain functions. Perhaps, Jules thought, some of them housed chickens. The train slowed to a crawl but there was nothing more to see. They were walled on both sides by mossy brick sidings and were soon entering the dark unwelcoming barn of Euston Station.

They were among the first off and sped along the platform hand in hand, passing a cluster of porters who were crying out to them even though they had no luggage. They separated from a wave of fearfully-erect dark-suited men carrying closed umbrellas and came to a stop at the Eversholt Street taxi rank. The cabby treated them as locals, referring to the new selling positions of the Tavistock Square newspaper boys as if Jules and Mr Wells were intimate with the previous selling positions used by the boys 'since time memorial.'

Inside the British Museum Jules' father expostulated about the anatomical verisimilitude of the equine half of the centaurs, which enabled him to ignore their human side altogether.[46] Jules had learned something about Spartans at school. He knew they were great warriors, as were King

Arthur and his knights. The sculptures helped him differentiate the Hellenic from the Britannic. Greeks did not dress as knights. They dressed in something resembling nighties, if at all.

Jules and his father left the centaurs to their defeat and made a quick tour of the Egyptian section. They stood before a cured cadaver with healthy-looking teeth. They ate in silence in a gloomy restaurant near Leicester Square, beside to two loud junior lawyers, former classmates, who worked for different firms. Jules touched the massive paws of a bronze lion in Trafalgar Square. All his preconceptions about the proportions of the world changed that day. He remembers three paintings at the National Gallery, Titian's *Allegory of Prudence*, Cézanne's *Bathers*, and El Greco's *The Agony in the Garden of Gethsemane*.[47] He learned that Agony comes from the Greek Agon, struggle, and that El Greco suffered from an eye disease. They wandered down Charing Cross Road and when Jules expressed an interest in a book about Greek sculpture Mr Wells bought it for him saying that about never regretting it.

When they returned his mother wasn't smiling. She had been afraid. His father drove the car home, the three of them across the front seat, Jules in his mother's embrace.

Later he wrote a letter to Cézanne. He still has the letter. She saved it for him. His mother kept it in her box of special memories, which came to him after she died.

When he opened it he understood a lot of things about his mother, he knew her in death as he had never known her in life. The letter was among her sacred objects, rosary beads, a tiny ivory crucifix, and a few reproductions, four centimetres by seven, of colossal counter-reformation works. Such cards used to fill her prayer book to bursting. On the reverse were prayers, professionally printed, with headings like *RIP* and *In Memoriam*, all that connected a dispersed family. Her own confirmation card was in there, a reproduction of a white-veiled virgin, palms pressed together in prayer, eyes raised towards heaven. An archaic, curlicue-loving hand had written her name, her new, completed name. She was now Elizabeth Mary *Cecilia* O'Rourke, confirmed in the Chapel of Coolagh, Feast of the Assumption, 15 August 1934.

The letter he had written was a question. He was always asking them. It was full of grammatical errors, so he can't have had any help in writing it:

Dear Mister Sezan, I only want to know? were are those bathers are going to.

His mother found a reproduction of *The Bathers* at the local library. She pointed to the two departing bathers and said, 'They are going bathing, I suppose.' And Jules felt a great mystery clearing up. 'Of course!' he repeated, imitating his father's manner, 'Bathing!' She never saw the original. She never went to the National Gallery. The extent of her interest in art was a Ptolemaic map of Hibernia on the wash-house wall taken from a National Geographic. When he was very small he was sure that she, not his expostulating father, knew everything. What is he sure of now? That a mother is like a second memory. That he was loved by one in whose eyes he was faultless.

∞

Entering the sculpted archway into the protection of the cathedral he is transported to a time when entering a church was itself an act of faith. Who would have thought it possible to construct such a roof? Swift said it was a brave man who ate the first oyster, but it was a braver one who ventured under the first vaulted ceiling.[48]

The space itself contributes to the purgatorial hubbub. Flocks of tourists circulate, whispering and scuffling.

Echoes dart and dissipate, shaped by the dimensions of the interior, taking on some of the hardness of its stone. Jules follows the right-hand aisle to a barrier from where he can inspect the northern rose. As another group overtakes him, the flash of a camera centimetres away sends him reeling. A woman apologises as his sight returns. He finds a quiet corner beside a disused confessional box where he raises his wounded bulbs to the last, the southern rose window. And the wagon-wheel sings. Fuelled directly, its deepest tones are raised from their sleep, and matter is exiled. The vaulted ceiling defies gravity, the stained glass window defies the materiality of stone. A figure approaches who knows him well.

'So. Let's go, professor.'

'Where to?'

'Back where you came from, till we reach the void.'

The first thing he sees on leaving the cathedral is a courageous child offering pieces of bread to birds which hover and strike at will. Pont St Louis is beyond the child. The flood seems to be drawing him towards it. Should he throw himself in...?

He throws himself in. He climbs onto the ledge in full view of some tourists and splashes into the icy current, diving, swimming as best he can in his overcoat and tweeds towards the bottom, kicking with all his might to nuzzle himself into the mud and glass and bangles of the river bottom. He is like a puppy nosing at the paps of its mother or a tadpole feeding off microscopica on algae leaves, wagging its tail merrily. See! Professor Wells is nose-down, kicking like an irate ass, head and shoulders buried in the mire, lungs filling with slime!

I was wretched, and yet that wretched life I still held dearer than my friend.[45]

He is staring at the mystery of the water when he hears a voice, a beggar appealing to him for money. His words seem to share Jules' own etymology in the dark flow. They touch him, as those of the Angel of the Annunciation touched the Virgin, and he reaches into his pocket. The beggar's heart skips a beat when he sees the 20 Euro note. The tourists are intrigued. A tour guide can't conceal her annoyance that he should encourage the tramps in this way. As Jules is holding it out, a small craft with a tall, sail-less mast glides towards them with the current.

It is the Ship of Fools from the painting by Hieronymous Bosch.[49] The mast-climber leaps up onto the eastern side of the bridge, bounds over to Jules and swipes the note. While the boat is passing underneath, he prances about in a wide circle, legs splayed and arms in the air like a conducting lobster. He has a long glistening knife and is grinning, grimacing at the others on the bridge who are heedless of his presence. He comes to Jules again and snips a button from his overcoat, which pops onto the pavement and bounces towards the river. He then leaps up on the western balustrade and reclaims his position at the top of the hazel branch mast when it reappears. As in the painting, he raises his knife towards a bound and roasted swan.

Jules enters the House of Photography and sways before a series of gelatin dayshades. Just a centimetre left or right is enough to lose the image. That is how daguerreotypes behave, or as we behave before them. The images have all suffered some damage caused by poor storage or handling. In the basement gallery is a show of newly discovered photographs from around the time the Seine flooded in 1910. Water pours down the entrance steps, flooding the early metro lines. The following year the river's banks are walled up and cemented. The mayor poses beside the workmen, proud of the latest anti-flood measures. Still the river claims the lower levees. It welcomes hats, branches of trees, articles of clothing. It is wild with whirlpools, rich with reflections. In the foyer are some Magnum photographs. Jules was at the opening, the opining, 'So moving!' 'So relevant!' 'So timely a retrospective!' 'How photography itself has been changed!' Seeing a woman weeping at the poignancy of an image of disillusioned communists, Jules offered her his handkerchief, of which he has a providential supply. He had no weeping in him. The death of his father and mother in quick succession had maimed his tear ducts.

When he steps outside all has changed. The path, the trees around about, everything seems to have been dipped in the river and lifted out again. Along the quai de l'Hotel de Ville the coursing storm-water, the dripping bridges, the moist stone, the sweating trees are simmering in a brilliant-edged aftermath, flickering, as if from within, at a fantastic rate. It is as if the planet has secreted. A team of tourists is posing for a photograph. Is it to remind themselves later, once they have been repatriated, of their collective displacement now? Is it to recall their shared knowledge of having visited a place they could never know? What exactly is the function of the world's impending positives? There are more negatives being exposed at any moment in hand-held cameras in Paris than all the surviving daguerreotypes in France. It is possible that in another hundred years only those daguerreotypes will have been preserved.

Two wide windows open on the second floor of the Hotel de Ville, as if the citizens are being offered access to the offices of power. A little fresh air, at least, is being allowed in. Jules passes a group of Tibetan monks, bald, robed impeccably, serried for a photograph in descending height before their touring van. The sight of them gives him the disturbing feeling that he has seen, just this morning, in the periphery of his vision or far off in the distance, another group of religious gentlemen, not saffron Buddhists, but an octet of dark-hooded pall bearers.

Businesswomen, tourists, teetotallers and bureaucrats pass Jules, some intended husbands and wives, some intended before their conception, some the result of an inattention to prophylaxy. Jules hears a loud hailer, a voice from inside a police car. Jules thinks of his own microphone, of his use of it, that he must learn how to use the new protective shields.

In the early days, the microphone was a cumbersome affair. He recorded the radio broadcasts of himself at home, with another microphone, circular, plastic, pressed against the loudspeaker of his gramophone. The radio signal in those days had the added charm of shifting into a soup of static-loaded voices belonging to other frequencies and occasionally other languages. Later, with the eighties came

FM, and unwanted sounds like discordant strings. Then he came to Paris and Yassim, a technical wizard, who records all Jules' emissions and cleans them of all unwanted whistles. It is Yassim who has told Jules he really should use the latest advance in microphone shields. They preserve intimacy more than the early foam rubber ones the colour of vomit.

[EXIT JULES, MUSING ABOUT MICROPHONE SHIELDS. ENTER EIGHT HOODED MOURNERS IN BLACK CLOAKS, CHANTING.]

Philippe Pot, Lord High Steward, Grand Seneschal of Burgundy, Knight of the Golden Fleece, Chamberlain to Louis XI and Charles VIII, ordered his tomb. Eight mourners carrying heraldic shields denoting his fiefs were to support on their shoulders an inscribed stone slab bearing his recumbent effigy. He was to be depicted in armour, at his pointed feet a watchful dog with visible claws. He watched it taking shape over the course of six years. Ten years after its completion, he was interred beneath it.[50]

In Paris with his father, the night after he first saw the work, the boy Jules woke in his room, short of breath and sweating profusely. He heard a thump. His father entered and fell asleep in his clothes. Jules couldn't sleep. He relieved himself in the hand-basin and went to the window to watch a whore on the street. Taxis and a straining nightbus passed. He thought of his mother at home with her new washing machine. He descended the stairs to the reception area. He did not dare to go outside. Just before dawn his father wheezed and groaned before falling silent as death. Their voices, hardly distinguishable from the noises of the night, were high and thin, like those of castrati. Their robes had seemed too big for them, as if they had ransacked the wardrobes of their fathers.

Last night, a third of a century later, they crossed Quai du Louvre after a night bus had rumbled by. They shared the dawn with some hospitable alcoholics under Pont Carrousel. All morning long, they have been weaving among family groups, fellow monks and the inevitable lovers, traversing open spaces, wandering unobserved through department stores, passing directly through walls and threading metro stations from end to end. Where the station has seemed fitting they have formed a group to bow and pray or to sing:

> *Where, oh where can he be?*
> *Where, oh where is our lord?*

Can Jules really be their required, this day of watermark, he who has gone out, 'out avisedness', tidelike?[51] In formation regular, of movement adamant, if tardigrade, in the jet garb of protectors of the secrets of medicine, poisons, gardening and pigments, the would-be bearers, bereft guardians of the seigniorial demesne, chant:

> *Wherefore is he absent from the bower?*
> *What are his drinks?*
> > *Sure, the Electropolitan*
> > *and the brandy liqueur.*
>
> *We would have him*
> *by the dark lily and the amaranth*
> *by seal, laserprint and paperweight.*
> > *Ours by right of aegis*
> > *lord to whom beholden.*
>
> *For him would we*
> *rally should menace arise*
> *for him quell with needful force*
> *insurrection in the wapentake.*
> > *For him censure by rood and rod*
> > *those forgetful of fealty.*
> *Lord to whom each is bound.*
> > *Lord who will protect us*
> > *from the silent evil of peace.*

Crush the violet!
Blast the primerole!
> *Bring the dominant blood to our hearts*
> *heat of his pipe to our lips!*

Where, oh where, is Jules?

The absquatulating rector of the monkey order has found himself a bench in a honey-basted park. A clown is leaning with a cowboy air against a dormant puppet booth, reciting lines to himself. A gardener is hoeing the helianthus ahead of season. If her form is upborne by her mind, like the form of the gardener in Shelley's *The Sensitive Plant*, it testifies to a highly muscular mental apparatus. Has a new ideal of woman been born? She is hoeing about white dog-roses in full maturity. They have a wild air, not like the ones Jules' father cultivated, not at all. His roses were the result of so much genetic engineering only self-fertilisation was possible. They were perfect, but their scent was unconvincing. The scent of these roses fills Jules with delight. He can only agree, with Sappho, that the rose is 'queen of the flowers.' He leans his head back in the cup of his hands, exclaiming to himself, 'Paradise!' The teacher in him adds,

'From the Persian *pairidaeza*, walled garden.'

Like all gardens, this one is threatened from within. Some clusters of Parisian buildings conceal gardens within. At the time when every prince in Europe dreamed of having his little Versailles, these were ideal places for intrigues such as those in *The Marriage of Figaro*. They were also evocative playgrounds for such bosky enchantments as those in *A Midsummer Night's Dream*. In contrast to the modern park, they included rendezvous points, copulation enclosures and even masturbation corners. Not so here, lovers must kiss openly by day and the gates are locked at dusk to prevent nocturnal trysts.

He stretches out his legs, resting the balls of his heels against the leather seam that his shoe-horn knows intimately. Johnston and Bros. A fine example of their functionality, durability and exquisite form. His heels have worn away again at 45°, the left heel to the left side, the right to the right. He wiggles his toes, he wiggles his toes, he wiggles his toes. They are stiff in the tendon, and cold in the bone, but he wiggles them, happy as a virgin *hortus conclusus*.

To his right is a sunlit wall. Nacreous trails traverse the former arterial routes of dead ivy. It is a vast history of imprints, fossils and dried slime. A beetle clambers, a woodlouse circles, a spider zigzags, all perpendicular to the earth. Vegetation too, colour, everything contravenes the downwards pull of gravity. The virginous green of the trees explodes, cork-coloured gloves of winter-sueded buds split open, new growth pushes, bees in the borage shove, svelte bronze fennel feathers motion. The flavour of spring explodes in his sinuses, petiole and blade resurrect in the heart. He would mix light yellow cadmium with pthalocyanine green and silvery-white.

On Sundays, when the vicar's improvisations failed to hold his attention, Jules used to slip into the universe of an allegorical stained-glass window above the nave. A black Roman soldier holding a spear was standing next to Veronica, who, for some years, Jules believed was Mary, Christ's mother. His own mother never converted to Anglicanism. She went to her own church during the week for confession. It had candles you could light for a penny and a painting so covered with grease it was difficult to make out its grieving forms.

And at the same time as oils were generating inner light and a sense of volume previously unknown, the painters' understanding of perspective developed a scientific basis. The iconic subjects of Christian art developed an inner as well as a celestial light as all around them landscapes effloresced and receded, bathed in divine hues and referential shadows.

When he opens his eyes, a slug is on the path. It has seized its moment to escape from a pile of freshly pulled weeds in quest of a hospitable, cold, dark rock. Otherwise typical of its species, this slug is more slimy than most. Measuring about seven centimetres by two, it retains the colour of the earth around about, and is heedlessly slow. It is oblivious to the sole of Jules' shoe, as it is to the clattering of a pair of ravens in the upper branches, who might pick off a gastropod purely for sport.

Jules understands immediately that this tongue-like foot sporting a modish nutty carapace scar is going in the wrong direction if it hopes to spend any more cosy nights under damp dirty ledges. Jules' father used to say creatures in the garden that move quickly are to be encouraged, those which move slowly are 'undesirable' and should be 'exterminated'. Considering that his closest encounter with death was due to the poison of a beautiful fast-moving South American spider, and considering that no slug, however adipose or vile to the touch, has ever been under his shirt or done him any direct harm whatever, he sees no reason to engage the precept. However loathsome, this miracle of creation has a right to its place in the liefdom of life under the astral cupola. How similar to man is the slug, *le limace*, as the French have aptly call it, so similar to the *limus terrae* of the scriptures, the 'slime of the earth' from which the body of man was created. The wake of slime exuded by the subject muscle, tinfoil silver, it is not dissimilar to certain human secretions. He could draw this as he learned to draw tears. He takes out his sketch pad and slowly the slime trail and the beast itself take shape. He has almost finished shading the carapace when a horde of stamping schoolchildren bursts through the gates. He defers, stretches out his leg and flicks Slug into the verdant garden where it will lie for a time camouflaged, motionless, looking more like a possum dropping than a member of the mollusc clan.

The horde of children gravitates to the puppet booth and surrounds the clown. Jules gazes up through a trellis of greening branches which, together with some ominous clouds punched here and there with aluminium pocks, prevent him from telling exactly where the sun lies. Some of the children hie off like a gaggle of goading elves. One finds Jules and gawks at him. She has seen his type, wizards some of them. You have to be careful, it is impossible to tell which ones might want to cut you up into mincemeat. An older child takes her by the hand and leads her back to the clown who is introducing the piece. When he finishes, the puppets, whose heads were lying lifelessly on the booth stage, are raised from the dead, appearing to move of their own accord. Jules is astonished, as the children are. He had not seen the clown's accomplices. He would like to remain astonished, as the children are, wide eyed, open-mouthed. And when they begin to giggle, shout, hooray, boo, hiss, and applaud out of hand, he would like to do that too, to be so very out of hand.

A witch turns a troubadour into a carrot because she doesn't like his singing. She locks a princess in a tower because she is jealous of her golden locks. She causes a baker and a butcher to argue to the point. They arrange a duel of fire against steel.

The children have been screaming from fear and clapping with relief, but now it is the night before the duel and they fall silent. At that moment a small bird, executioner of smaller prey, servant of the colour code, reconnoitrer of sexual or hierarchical networks, spins down in wheels and stations itself in mid-air before Jules. From the centre of a sickening blur created by its desperately beating wings, two tiny dark eyes in a symmetrical, motionless head fix him. Its beak has become a lethal protuberance just centimetres from Jules' own nose. He dares not blink lest it think his eyelashes are the legs of a savoury centipede. Some desert birds are given to pecking out the eyes of dying men. Who is to say this is not one of them? See! It is not a harmless Parisian bird at all. It has something Saharan about it. The head is Egyptian, no question. And those eyes, spiteful, fateful! The locals in his village had a bird-scaring call, 'Shoo! Shua! all ye birds. Hilly Ho!' Should he try it? Might it not have the reverse effect?

Meanwhile, a frog overhears the witch's secret while she is collecting scum from his pond. The frog is then captured by a cook who is about to cut off his legs. The clown asks the audience, should he cut off the frog's legs? The children raise such a cry in reply that the bird is gone in a flash. Jules is grateful to them. He blinks slowly, to warm and moisten his eyeballs. The frog buys his freedom with the information he possesses about the witch — she is afraid of the dark. A kindly giant puts a black hood over the witch and makes her undo the evil she has done. The frog turns into a prince. The troubadour sings at the royal wedding.

The children, set free from the performance, scream and disperse. They venture close to Jules.

'Are you the man who turns children into sausages?'

He peers down his nose and puts on a Transylvanian accent, 'I'm the one who turns them into grown-ups!'

They run back to spread the news about the wizard on the bench as the teachers do their best to round them up. In fact, cannibalism was not far from his thoughts. During Henry IV's siege of 1590, when there were no more domestic pets to eat, some children were, reportedly, served up, perhaps on this very spot.

Slug, meanwhile, has found his way back on to the path out of Jules' leg-reach. The teachers have established order and are leading the children in unruly file by the long route under the plane trees. They are singing to the tune of Three Blind Mice:

> *Slip slap slug*
> *tick tack clowning*
> *up the garden and downing*
> *a contradiction in terms of the law*
> *an invertebrate dinosaur*
>
> *A big bad bug*
> *a sick sad frowning*
> *a slithery rubber a browning*
> *no house not even a door*
> *bad to behold such a bore*

Dig dag dug
not the model ideally
a letter without a sincerely
not the tooth of a carnivore
a big mess on the floor

The last of the children spits behind him, a sly silent cream without parabola. It is like a tongue itself, an attribute of the boy's throat, darting to ground. The boy follows the line of other children into the milky shades that cover them all in a silky wrapping, legs protruding. Feeling an itch under his own belly-veil, Jules surrenders and scratches. A little dog enters the park leading a pensioner. The dog is sprightly, nose alert. Jules has a sudden fear of this doggie, of all little Paris doggies. What if they turned on his odour with their underused teeth? A man might be mauled. He gets to his feet. A raven caws. The clown undresses. Jules leaves the seat and picks his way through the remains of slugs out of the park. As the gate bashes back on its spring, he takes the direction opposite to that taken by the children. By the church of St Julien le Pauvre he checks again the hastily sketched map. The cross must represent the Cluny Museum.[52] And there, that must be the café in question. A rainbow flag, faded and dusty, is hanging outside.

Some tables are laid for lunch. The one he chooses is situated between the inset door and a windowed extension. Two men nearby are speaking quietly, like civilised gentlemen, though there is something conspiratorial about their manner.

'Allowing them to marry and have children was transmitting the defective gene, see.'

'But won't it be easier for them to become parents later on, you know, with adoption and artificial insemination and all that?'

'We'll legislate against it once we've got enough seats. The church is still on our side and the electoral process will swing our way, I'm sure of it. It's the law of averages. Le Pen was almost president, wasn't he? We'll get this faggot out of the town hall and fix 'em for good.'

They take their coats solemnly as a pair of punks who have been leaning on the bar head for the empty table. They rumble the chairs out and settle in, extending holed, rotting sneakers. The skin around the lip stud of one of them is inflamed. Jules touches his own lip with the tip of his tongue. He prefers their company to that of the homophobes, but nature is calling to him to descend the spiral staircase. He tells himself the jet is stronger than yesterday though it is the usual dribble. He scrutinises his bowl-waters. No blood. No alarm — though who can say what surgical analysis would reveal. Some 15th century painters attended autopsies. Antonio Pollaiuolo was the first to study anatomy by dissection.[53] The swelling of the archer's veins in his St Sebastian testifies to it. He was, by occupation, a layer of gold-leaf upon flat surfaces. He and his brother were sons of a poultry merchant, another form of dissector, so they had probably known the secrets of chicken anatomy since childhood. Leonardo da Vinci waited for a centenarian to die so he could draw the tubes responsible for his excellent circulation. At art school Jules could hardly wait for that part of the course, with its laying bare of sanguinary and urinary apparatuses, to be over. He prefers living models, and unruptured skin.

He squirts a dollop of pink soap into his cupped hands and the dirt of his day spirals away in umber streaks. The washroom is screaming with brilliant fluorescent light, which makes its walls of cobalt and quinacridone magenta tawdry. On his return to the table, the punks are unfolding maps and discussing what to do next. Sonja, the Lorenzetti Virgin, is sipping coffee on the other side of the café. She is alone by the inner wall. Neither she nor Jules are where they said they would be at two o'clock. The waiters busy themselves with the lunchtime orders. One of them asks

Jules discreetly, 'Are you Professor Wells?'

'I am.'

He hands him an envelope. 'You want something else?'

'An Evian.'

Jules opens it. It says simply, '3pm.' Two policemen on street duty order ham rolls and idly check out the poker machine at the back of the bar. The punks sneer in their direction. Sonja has had unpleasant experiences with police at demonstrations. She finishes her cigarette and does up the buttons of her suede coat. On her way out she notices Jules and deviates towards him. 'I just wanted to say that I don't agree with you at all.'

'Miss Kaufmann!'

'An artist's health has nothing to do with his formal choices.' Her spectacles are more spectacular than ever. Her fingernails are painted deep wine, her fingers stained black with printing ink. Her shoulder-line shows through the retro muslin of her Veronese-green blouse.

'I don't follow.'

'Look at the empirical evidence. Look at the work of artists with HIV. Every generation has its incurable diseases and its epidemics. Everyone is told, sooner or later, that he is about to die. But artists face death every day. Epidemic or accident, they work among it, in the face of it.'

Her hair is lightly troubled, not professionally so. Her right hand is impatient, her fingers search for words in the Italian manner.

'I'm not saying that those things you talked about, miniaturism or fascination-with-the-bovine... I'm not saying they have nothing to do with illness. Perhaps art really did begin with the power of the living to destroy life... with descriptions of the hunt, or of warriors receiving their wounds... or in grieving, you know... in remembering the dead, or in wishing to be remembered yourself! But we can't know whether the sun will rise on us in one week's time. Artists put their fingers into the mud, don't you think? Writers, too, they dare, at least they try ... to overcome the semantic disturbances ... the ones that happen when we falsely believe we have understood reality. All artists are fighting... not dying! ... fighting against all who claim power over reality because they have structured its appearance, because they have drawn the map! But the map is not the thing mapped, is it, professor?'

He twitches his eyebrows at her. She leans an elbow on the three-legged table which rises slightly on two of its feet. She doesn't want an answer. She just wanted to have her say.

'So we've had our meeting after all,' he ventures.

'Shall we have another?'

'If you like. I am not offering 'The Design of Illness' next year. If you are staying in Paris for the holidays, I'll need a researcher for my new series of lectures.'

'Yes, I will. Yes, of course. Thank you.'

'We could meet here at the same time next week. That'll be better than my office.'

'No. I... my boyfriend is visiting me next week.'

Jules does not falter. 'Two weeks from Monday, then... in the department.'

They shake hands and he watches her go before calling to the waiter for a glass of house wine. He recalls Owens singing in mid-flight, *'Tis woman that seduces all mankind*,[54] a self-interested assertion, not unrelated to the fact that Owens is homosexual. He once said that all house wine in cafés is poison, though he later retracted. He still insists there is always a very good bottle on the wine list and quite a poor one and they will both have the same price; and if you trouble the waiter to recommend one he will give you the only good bottle with a bad cork.

On one occasion when I was troublesome to my master Rembrandt, by asking him too many questions concerning the causes of things, he replied very judiciously: try to put well in practice what you already know; in so doing you will, in good time, discover the hid-

den things which you now enquire about.[55]

'Hoogstraaten was a great deceiver. He deceived an emperor and won a medallion, which he reproduced in his paintings of paintings of letter racks. How they died for a good fooling, the collectors! What do they die for now? For a pilfered sketch? For a city?'

'You are a Calaitian in spirit, perhaps?'[56]

'No, not for Calais. I wouldn't die for any city.'

'Rodin wanted to be buried in the mausoleum of his Tower of Work.'[57]

'And so, in a sense, he was.'

'And so are all workers, from sculptors to bakers.'

'Nimrod's archers fired arrows from the Tower of Babel into heaven. Angels caught them in their hands and threw them back with blood on them. He believed he had killed the angels and conquered heaven.'

'We are the same. Doubly deluded.

'A man tried to fly.'

'From Babel?'

'From Eiffel.'

'He flew?'

'He fell. It's on film. Straight as a plumb.'

'He fell into film, then.'

'Into the flickering light.'

'What would you flicker for?'

'For another wine.'

'Aren't you going to eat that sandwich?'

'Would you? Look lively, the waiter!'

'Very good. Same again, please.'

'No need for compliments. A tip, that is enough. Quality is assumed.'

'As with roses.'

'You sent her a rose for every performance.'

'A plant in a pot once.'

'Carried in the correct manner.'

'The seducee is to carry the pot under his arm with the blooms protruding.'

'Not in a plastic bag from any cash and carry!'

'But the roses — were they gift-wrapped?'

'On every occasion.'

'Low score! Predictable. The decorum of roses, like life, has exceptions. *The unwrapped rose may, in certain circumstances, signify spontaneity, as if plucked on an irrepressible whim.*'

'I never gave her an unwrapped rose.'

'She must have had her doubts.'

'She was free. She wasn't another man's wife.'

'Praiseworthy in another time! You should have thought

about seducing another man. Such as the one who was busy seducing her.'

'My toes are numb.'

'Toes are the first to go. Better to give up the tobacco.'

'You feel the toes after they have been amputated, as you never did before. Sometimes they itch and you cannot scratch them. Or there is an aching pain in the space they no longer occupy. The pain of amputation arrives later, the pain from which anaesthesia protected you.'

'I only smoke out of doors or at open windows. It's my way of cutting down.'

'Bigger shoes. Death is always taking its soundings. There are other symptoms.'

'Such as talking to yourself?'

'That's harmless. You're only keeping in touch with your best friend. "When we are perfectly reconciled, we are silent." Virginia Woolf. Toothache gone?'

'Still there, in a space I continue to occupy.'

'If you place your head beside a gatepost, and your mother strikes the gatepost with a hammer, either the toothache will stop or the tooth will fall out.'

'The Somerset cure.'

'But you aren't to trust anyone other than your mother with the task, he or she might be 'lacking' or 'not exactly' and crack your skull open by mistake.'

'The toothache would go.'

'Along with existence.'

'Shualy Shoo!'

TOGETHER: *'Shua O! Shua O!*
Shoo, shoo, shoo!
Hilly ho!'

As Jules and his self are dancing a two-step on the side plate to the Mendip bird-scaring call, a renovation team on an upper floor sends bricks, tiles and plaster down sleeved buckets to a wide bin on the street causing clouds of plaster-dust to flare in the sunlight.

'Turner loved clouds and anything resembling them. Steam trains huffing and puffing over the county buttercups.'

'He was like a steam train himself.'

'He had enormous feet.'

'One foot in the eighteenth, in the nineteenth he legged it with a Mrs Bloom. While living with her he was known to the neighbours as Mr Bloom.'

'Another happy artist!'

Part of the park on the other side of the street is

screened off by a placard containing an architect's representation of the medieval garden being created within.

'In imitation of a garden in imitation of The Garden.'

'Huysman's. Chapter eight. Des Esseintes seeks blooms that look like fakes.'

The sun is obscured by a ream of clouds. All ornament and order loses its wideband.

'The Tower of Siloe crushed eighteen workmen when it collapsed.'

'God will crush us in the same way if we do not repent.'[58]

Rain clouds are thickening overhead.

'Crushing and stoning were ever popular.'

'Look at St Stephen.'

'The woman taken in adultery.'

'Camillus in the painting by Poussin.'[59]

'There's a foul-up if ever there was one.'

'Phidias had nowhere to run either. He was thrown in prison where he died, some say poisoned.'[60]

'Happens to the best of us.'

'And the worst!'

The Woman with a Doe has been observing Jules with interest. She plants herself down in the chair opposite him. Her eyes never leave his face. They move quickly over its surface, measuring its reactions. He examines her in return. Her skin is badly scarred, pitted like the surface of the moon. Her eyelids are red, sleepless.[61] The coffee cup seems ridiculously small, breakable in her grasp.

'Thanks for the envelope.'

'Sure. Can you buy me a sandwich?'

'Go ahead. Do you know where I live as well?'

'Relax, Professor Wells, no one's going to get hurt.'

'And your boyfriend?'

'My son.'

'He can't go on getting his face smacked in.'

'What do you care. He can't eat his good looks.'

Jules has no answer. He looks uncomfortable. She changes tack: 'It was good of you to help him.'

'It was two onto one.'

'Fair play. How English. You cared. Nice. But you know, if you really want to help, it's not pity we need, it's money.'

'Success has a lot to do with luck. You could do with some of that, perhaps.'

She leans back and runs her eyes over him rudely. She sees a middle-aged man whose hair is falling out. The pocket of his suit jacket is gaping open. The end of his pipe is too-much loved, too chewed. 'What do you know about success?'

He holds his ground. 'You need to get to know people.'

'So? I'm getting to know you.'

He finds the invitation to André Vidal's new gallery. 'It's good for two persons.'

'Oh! Really?'

'I was going to go but... a friend is in town.'

'English?'

'French. You see, Vidal.'

'I mean your friend, is he English?'

'Yes. English. So what?'

'We tried to get in there.'

'England?'

'They turned us back.'

'Why England?'

'I ask myself.'

She flicks the edge of the invitation. 'I don't get it.'

'There'll be journalists, artists, buyers, hunters and collectors, you know?'

'Didn't you notice? We do metro carriages.'

'So get to know someone influential. A banker, a filmmaker. You never know what it will lead to.'

'So that's it!'

'What?'

'Some kind of score to settle?'

'No score! I'm thinking of you!'

'Sure. They'll throw me out. Look at me.'

'Some students don't look any different from you. You'll be fine.'

She takes the invitation and gets to her feet. 'I'll see you tonight.'

'I won't be there, I told you.'

She slides the invitation into an ammunitions pocket, saying coldly, 'Paris is not as big as you think it is, Professor Wells.' As she melts into the passing crowd, a premature gloom sets in. Some dollops of rain splash like paste from a pail against the window. The rainbow lies again. The punks are considering taking a look at *The Lady and the Unicorn*: 'A tapestry?'[62]

'You never heard of it?'

'I think so.'

'There are some cool crucifixions, too.'

Jules follows at a discreet distance to the entrance of the museum. He shows his professorial card to a security guard who waves him through. He passes a derelict well and enters the crucifixion room. He crosses a gallery of medieval pilgrimage merchandise where the punks are giggling uncontrollably. He climbs a set of stairs above the Roman baths. Some fifteenth century statues of mourning mothers glide by before he arrives at the lecterns where some brass framed pages of several Books of Hours and Days are displayed. One is open at the month of May. The sign of naked twins in a small golden oval is opposite a stiff candidate on a horse. The caption reads, *The Lord departs for the falcon hunt.*

A siren passes.

On his way out Jules has another look at the Lady and her beast. Their saga of survival has always endeared the tapestry to him. The compelling vanity of the one-horned one made 'Vision' a favourite. The Lady is fatigued, disappointed, gazing at the unicorn who is admiring itself in her bejewelled golden-framed mirror. The punks arrive.

'It's not a carpet, dildo!'

'It's too dark, you can't see a thing.'

'Wait for your eyes to adjust.'

'It's like the chamber of horrors. Hey! You could get away with murder in here!'

Jules glides from the museum feeling like a rosined bow on new strings, effortless, cadence-rich with freed motion. He no longer finds the noises of the city annoying, they have become joyous ejaculations. Faces, in whose gauntness he had seen only lines of strain, now reveal the glint of secret hopes and guarded joys. Rounding the corner of boulevard St Michel and boulevard St Germain he bumps into Fleur. Her mobile phone falls from her hand. To Jules she is the mistress of Henry II, École Française.[63]

> *What strange reversals*
> *here operate*
> *I with my arrows and arched brows*
> *you with your brushes*
> *and sorrows.*
>
> *You're bound to disguise*
> *my shortened spine*
> *with lengthened legs*
> *of creamy flesh*
> *shoulders and belly*
> *born to carry*
> *breasts yet to lactate.*
>
> *Make good your god-greedy wish*
> *in oil and cloth!*
> *Night and day await*
> *the sweat of him who swore his troth*
> *to fornicate!*

Her mobile phone hits the pavement. He scoops it up.

'It's you, sir.'

'I wasn't looking where I was going.'

'Me neither!'

'I'm glad I ran into you! I ... I...'

Jules is only too aware of the impropriety of talking to a prostitute in the street. Fleur saves him, 'Were you wanting to do some drawings?'

'Splendid! Yes!'

'It's so much fun. I can bring a friend this time. She's like you asked for, big, you know, but not fat.'

'How about next week, next Monday, then. Early evening. Say around 5:30?'

'I'll say yes! Don't you worry. I'll manage it, professor!'

She winds through the pedestrian traffic, delighted, dialing the mobile phone with her thumb. No one but Jules can know she is communicating with a tall ageing pockmarked transsexual Brazilian known to clients as Madame Garonne. Another voice, other voices are talking into mobile phones. Is he the only person not dialling, confirming and cancelling? A shower of water sweeps over the street. There is an explosion of umbrellas before unsheltered shop frontages. A bookseller rushes to cover his stalls with plastic. A man cries out. A woman apologises.

'No, no, madam! Yes, I'm fine. Thank you.' The man is inspecting his handkerchief for blood. He invites the woman to lunch. They trot away, the points of her umbrella seeking other eyeballs.

If a physician with a bronze lancet opens an abscess in the eye of a man and destroys the man's eye, they shall cut off his fingers.[64]

'Is a painter responsible for the effect of his work? Francesco Francia died after seeing Raphael's Saint Cecilia. Was Raphael responsible for that?'

'It wasn't the painting that killed him. His life's work seemed trivial beside it.'

'He should have known. Art is a deception best appreciated by those familiar with the lineage of its formation.'

'Deception represented the profane. Holbein's Judas kiss.[65] Not a kiss, but a proximity.'

'You can almost smell his breath.'

'Jesus is hardly breathing, hardly human, the Divine made man, the Beautiful.'

'The double-cross awaits us all, with one surprise — we are ugly and beautiful, betrayer and betrayed.'

A woman passes through the rain, a magazine spread over her hairdo. She is tall, dark-skinned as Mélita was.

Mon bel amour, mon cher amour
Ma déchirure
Je te porte dans moi
Comme un oiseau blessé[66]

She boards a bus, one with light-reducing windows. Jules scrambles aboard and the journey passes as a dream. The passengers are characteristically quiet, but are prevented from engaging in their usual repertoire of discreet signs by the Cimmerian soup. Three stops later she descends. He lands on the pavement after her. Shoving, bustling, buying, trading reality floods in. As ever in the vicinity of railway stations, the professions of the women lose their clarity. A sex shop advertises English Education. He picks his way through the umbrellas. She is in a perfume shop. Among the cosmetics she opens a compact. Her finger-ends trip lightly, without examining, but verifying, seeing by touch. She passes her right hand over her face. It casts an emerald shadow over her tried skin. Jules takes a brochure advertising a nearby *centre de bronzage* from the counter. It says, "In Paris you can buy anything, even the sun." He looks around the shop as if he is looking for a gift. He goes to the compacts, to within scenting distance of her. She is trying to decide — pervert or prospect. A wash of golden light illuminates the interior of the shop. Neither is strictly true. She opts for pervert, snaps the compact shut, tosses it into the merchandise stand, and is gone out the doors to the next pass.

> *Et ceux-là sans savoir*
> *Nous regardent passer*
> *Répétant après moi*
> *Ces mots que j'ai tressés*
> *Et qui pour tes grands yeux*
> *Tout aussitôt moururent*
> *Il n'y a pas d'amour heureux.*[66]

He lifts his satchel over his head and finds the address. A sculpted stone doorway shades a vestibule with a personalised intercom for customers. He presses a button marked House of Health. A door clicks open.

'Good day, sir.'
'Your brochure.'
'You'll need to book.'
'I came on impulse. I have time just now.'

The manager is chemically tanned. She has huge sleepy cowls for eyelids but an accountant's eyes. 'The fact is, the sun-lamps are being serviced today. But the steam-bath is excellent. Gérard Depardieu recommended it. It's completely relaxing. And afterwards you take a warm soak.'

He drops his wallet and watch into a pea-green numbered pouch and perches on a wooden bench in the steam room. It is a contour-obliterating experience, a heat wave in a London fog. An attendant enters brusquely and throws a bucket of water on some kind of hot plate. The action makes him think of slops. He makes out the pencil-thin moustache of a lean Mediterranean type through the steam clouds.

'Hello again.'

Jules replies in his direction, 'We don't know each other, I don't think.'

'I have seen you, but you haven't seen me, perhaps. I'm sorry. I thought we knew each other already.'

'No, I have never seen you. I would have remembered.' Jules says this with assurance, though he can not see the man's face clearly at all. The man's voice comes out of the steam again:

'I'll be honest with you. I just wanted to talk. A friend of mine—'

'I sympathise but, you know, I need calm today. That's why I came here.'

'Yes, of course. Thank you.'

The heat and humidity are already too much for Jules. He goes next door for a bath. Each tub is big enough for four persons. His body fills a purple-plastic submarine support, leaving only the head above forty-degree water. Through the gently stirring haze he catches glimpses of a tropical paradise, sentimental, perverse. It is a copy of a painting by Jan Bruegel the Elder — Odysseus making love to his captor in her cave of sensual delights.[67] Calypso would have him for all time, but he has made up his mind to leave her. The paint is not suited to the environment. It never properly stuck to the wall. At each end of the room are Japanese sliding screens leading to the steam chamber and to a massage room. Little bubbles are rising from Jules' skin. A dead mosquito is bobbing on a rainbow oil slick. He hears a rushing sound as if millions of people are scraping their shoes inside his head ...

He hears a panting in the hallway, beast-like. It ends with a thump against the wall and a hurried whispering of voices. His father enters the darkened room, smelling of whisky and smoke and an unknown perfume. He collapses on the second bed. Jules lets the hours pass, mourning for his mother, for his father, for the whore on his fathers breath.

Up till the advent of psychoanalysis, the path of knowledge was always traced in that of a purification of the subject, of the per-cipiens. *Well! We would now say that we base the assurance of the subject in his encounter with the filth that may support him.*[68]

The Mediterranean type has entered the bath. Blood-warm currents are flowing from unseen jets near their feet. Jules drags himself out and wraps a towel around himself. He slides a panel open and is faced with a row of massage cubicles, some closed off by plastic curtains. A masseuse emerges from behind a screen wiping her hands and points to an operating table on rollers. She clicks a locking mechanism and asks him, 'You were wanting, sir?'

'The way out.'

The traffic around Sèvres-Babylone is jammed. A driver sounds his horn repeatedly. The others wait with an expression more blank than patient.

Man's life on earth is short and he cannot, by his own perception, see the connection between the conditions of earlier times and of other nations, which he has not experienced himself, and those of his own times, which are familiar to him.[45]

By way of compensation for 'the filth' that supports him, he writes a plot for the Woman with a Doe and her boy. They meet a film-maker who wants them in his film of the life of the painter Masaccio. The boy is perfect for the part. A bus approaches. The driver sees him late and sounds his horn. A hand grabs Jules' arm and pulls him back. An enamel-green and zinc-white avalanche streaks in one wide brush stroke before Jules. The bus lurches, passengers cry out, three adults and a foldable pushchair crash over an elderly passenger whose package crumples. Seeing no casualties, the driver accelerates away. A child watches Jules and his saviour from the rear window of the bus. Norma's hand is still clutching his arm.

'Safe and sound!'

'Yes. Oh! Yes!'

'You are very pale! Are you all right, professor?'

'I ... I think so.'

'A close call.'

'Yes. Close. What a fool I am!'

'It can happen to anyone. Especially in this city. There's the green man. Shall we cross over? You were thinking of something else, perhaps.'

'I was.'

'What was it?'

'I've forgotten.'

'It couldn't have been more important than your life. But you look like death itself. You should sit down for a moment.'

'No, I'm all right. It'll... it'll pass!'

'My rehearsal rooms are near here, we could go there or... I know a café just a skip away.'

'That would be very nice.'

'You don't smoke, do you?'

'Yes, I do, in a way.'

'That won't suit us then.'

'I'm giving up. It'll be fine.'

'But perhaps you need to smoke to calm yourself down.'

'Yes. You're right. I'll sneak a few puffs on the way.'

'Have you tried to give up before?'

'This is the first time.'

'I like Indonesian herbal cigarettes. Tried them?'

'I can't find them anywhere!'

'I'll ask the harpist. She smokes them.'

'You rehearse around here?'

'Behind Saint Sulpice. How's that cigarette?'

'Disgusting!'

'That's the spirit! There's the café, half way along on the left. You see it?'

The street and the footpath have narrowed so much that first Jules, then Norma, have to give way to other pedestrians coming from the other direction. Just before the entrance she runs into another musician.

'Near-death! Be a dear and explain for me, would you? Half-an-hour. He's had a terrible shock.'

The café is also a bookshop. Browsing is permitted, purchasing encouraged. The customer areas are painted in shades of deep green, the bar is decorated in purple and wood tones with horizontal lines of tubular steel.

'One concentration lapse and the piece is ruined. Sometimes we miss our cues, you know, and it's impossible to cover up, the way actors do. It can ruin a performance.'

'Yes, well, I hope I haven't ruined your day.'

'You've made it. Really! I've been so much wanting to have another chat with you.'

'I was afraid I bored you last time.'

'I'm not one to pretend, professor. Did you buy the painting, the one with all the senses?'

'No, no.'

'Were you disappointed?'

'I didn't have my heart set on it.'

'It might have been good for you. A beautiful object has a beneficial effect on the owner, don't you think? I have my cello!'

'I have an authentic engraving by a Dutch master.'

'I remember! You told me about it in the bus.'

'You must come and see it.'

'I'll do that. You won't forget you've invited me?'

'I'm not that fickle! Hey, you know, it's come back to me — what I was thinking of.'

'When?'

'When I walked in front of the bus.'

'Oh really?' Norma is still not sure whether she prevented an accident or a suicide.

He is about to tell her about the film he had been inventing in his head about the boy and his mother, but, afraid it might jeopardise relations, he exclaims instead, 'Potassium permanganate!'

'Oh, yes? Why were you thinking of that?'

'I don't know why. Royal colours!'

'Royal colours are blue aren't they?'

'Yes but... in Roman times they were... like potassium permanganate.'

'Oh yes?'

'And it changes its colour under different conditions.'

'As if it was... alive, like a chameleon!'

'You could say that.'

'Did you know that an onion... the tip of an onion root

will stimulate the tip of another root to grow more quickly?'

'I didn't.'

'And if you put an apple in a bowl of green avocados they ripen twice as quickly.'

'Incredible!'

'Contact between people gives us life as well, of course. It's going on all around us, professor.'

'Yes! Yes, of course!'

'Chance meetings, feelings, moods! We are all jostling and startled and startling bodies, wouldn't you say?'

'Absolutely!'

'Life is not logical, is it?'

'Not in the slightest.'

'It is crammed full of coincidences and worthwhile moments.'

'Our meeting proves it.'

'But we can influence what will happen, even the unimaginable, if we accept that there are conditions that make miracles more likely.'

'I believe it. There's more to the picture than meets the eye.'

Norma sips her tea with slow, oriental gestures, hands on either side of the cup.

'That's why I am a musician, professor — because nothing gives me greater pleasure than to play with other musicians. It keeps me well!'

'I see! Yes! But you must call me Jules. Didn't you just save my life? I would have been mincemeat!'

'Let's not think of that! Let's think of... that miniature.'

'With the senses?'

'The artist, who was it—?'

'I don't know. A group, perhaps.'

'They saw things visually, of course?'

'Of course.'

'They received it, all about the world, visually. Do you see what I'm getting at?'

'Not really.'

'They heard it visually, they smelt it visually, and so on. A writer... he sees and hears and tastes ...verbally. You see?'

'And you see and hear and taste everything musically, then?'

'That's it. Of course, there are degrees and I know everything isn't music, but I receive everything as music. There are musicians who hear everything as words. They should really be writers. Are you with me?'

'I am.'

'I think art can cure us, it can keep us well. Don't you?'

'Oh yes!'

'I used to think that art represents the world. But now I think that it is most occupied with breaking us free of the world. The world is a cage, whose door is forever closing on art. The arts are in constant danger. As musicians, we have to identify the current form of music's slavery. We have to admit that a lot of the tyranny is self-generating. We have to improve our technical skills so we can break free, purify the discipline and purify ourselves. Even though the moment we have struck the liberated chord, it will be trapped, branded, and chained. It is the best we can do to offer a moment of light, don't you agree?'

'I have a little oil lamp. It's an imitation of one found at Pompeii. I light it in the night.'

'Good. Yes, of course. The visible world, and the non-visible world. I see everything as music. That means the same thing. I would see your oil lamp as music. It is impossible for me to see or hear or smell or feel anything without rendering it audible. I transfer all shapes and impressions audible and inaudible, as they are received by all the senses, into sounds. As for you, your judges are ocular-privileged, vision experts. See?'

'So education counts for nothing.'

'It counts for everything! The important thing is to admit we are caged by its rudiments, its rules of counterpoint and modulation.'

'I hadn't thought of it that way.'

'You were thinking about that already.'

'Not in the same way! I hadn't pinpointed the problem. Except that—'

'Yes?'

'My lamp—'

'What about it?'

'The flame burns.'

'So?'

'It burned my hand this morning. You can't see anything, there isn't any blister, but I felt it. You're not saying I felt it visually, are you?'

'Yes, I am. Or in some mixed proportion of the privileged senses.'

'All right. I'll think more about it. I'd love to hear you play, the whole orchestra. I... the piece... the piece by Ravel... I couldn't get a ticket.'

'You were wanting to come?'

'I know your part note for note. And now I absolutely must see it... that is to say, hear it, of course!'

'Leave it to me. I'll let you know if I can manage it. But now I have to go. We're very busy this week. They'll be wondering where I am. Bye bye, professor.'

'Yes, of course. Bye bye!'

Her black hair is parted at the back, one of her ample arms is embracing the orchestral score of *Daphnis and Chloë*.

SECTION 187.
Very slowly.
Chloë falls into the arms of Daphnis.

A Madagascan funerary sculpture causes a Polish art student to cross the street for a closer look. Rare 18th century editions catch the eye of a transatlantic tourist returning to his hotel. A Japanese collector pauses along the narrow footpath to admire the latest acquisitions from Eastern Europe and the Middle East, shameless on their plinths. Jules' step hardly falters. The events of the day have all but cut him free from object-lust.

When he arrives at Au Chat Gris, Owens is on to his second Friar's Cocktail, topped with icy froth.

'You've lost a few kilos, Milo.'

'It was all fashion padding.'

'To deflation!'

It is more than a year since they last saw each other and Jules has indeed lost some weight. His suit hangs as if it really belongs to a bigger man, something Owens would never allow to happen. They move to a table on the pavement to perch on two undersized chairs. Owens has been travelling more than ever, taking in the Asian sub-continent, the Balkans and southern Italy. Jules has hardly budged except for a summer trip back to Somerset and a three-day conference in Cologne.

'There's a painting there in the Wallraf-Richartz-Museum.[69] A man and a leering child are crouched beside the bars of a street-level cell, making the two-fingered devil-sign behind a platform. On the platform is an accused prisoner. Behind the grill of the street-level cell is another prisoner. I am the prisoner behind the grill. What is my first name?'

'Is the accused prisoner on the platform both man and God.'

'There are those who say it.'

'So you must be Barabbas!'

'Yes. But what is my first name?'

'First name... must be... I don't know. I have never known that.'

'Jesus.'

'Jesus Barabbas?'

'Jesus, son of Abbas.'

'Oh yes! Very good!'

They invented the guessing game years ago as a way of combining their interests in criminology and art.

'I am a sign, a particular sign that prevents my wearer from being hanged.'

'What century are we in?'

'Your period. The Middle Ages. The person who is wearing me has committed a hanging offence. I am the sign that will get him off the hook.'

'You might be a shield... a heraldic sign, silver cups hanging from my saddle?'

'Close.'

'You win.'

'A haircut!'

'What?!'

'Monks were exempted from hanging, and they were identified by their tonsures.'

'Oh, yes! Early on that was true. Point! Your tonsure is nicely trimmed.'

'Yours is excellently neglected as ever!'

'I won't tell my barber you said that.'

'You have one?'

'In Somerset. And you? Haven't I ever told you that short hair was a sign of slavery among the Greeks. Do you have yours cut in London?'

'On the fifth of every month.'

'I've got one more, if you're game.'

'I'm always game.'

'A wintry night in 1455. The guards do not know my face, but they find my given name, Mouton, amusing. I don't have any papers, but I say I am leaving Paris on a family matter, and France not being at war, the guards let me pass into the anonymous dark, to the provinces and safety.'

'1455... Guillaume Dufay?'

'I have committed a crime. The only chance of asylum is disguise, the only chance of return is the written word, and something else, some proof of my innocence.'

'Visible proof?'

'Physical. I return with two letters of remission, from François des Loges in Paris and from François de Moncorbier of Saint Pourçain near Moulins where the king is in residence.'

'And the physical proof?'

'A scar on my lip.'

'A priest! You killed a priest?'

'Perhaps. All right.'

'Villon! François Villon!'[70]

Jules congratulates Owens. They toast themselves and head for the restaurant. As they are tracking along Quai

Voltaire, the sun finds the lower edge of the cloud layer, which gleams with a marigold trim. The last illuminations of day ignite the heavy undersides of the clouds. As the gloaming achieves its most brilliant moment, the stone of the Louvre seems to be beaming, shining with its own light. Then, a few seconds later, it is over — the Jardin des Tuileries retires behind a screen of black rubber stretched to the limit of its elasticity. Caretakers are gesticulating and shouting to all newcomers that they are closing up. Eight unemployed pall-bearers utter a forsaken cry, such as that which will precede the last trumpet. Their plain chant rises into the sonic blur of the city. The words are printed across the city's clouds of unknowing in violet lettering:

> *Over-riding changes*
> *will be overridden*
> *new means of writing*
> *underwritten.*

> *Where clear water flows*
> *mortality flies*
> *where dark water grows*
> *vitality hies.*

At that moment, the boy who looks like Masaccio and his mother are staking out the terrain at André Vidal's new gallery. They do not know the rules of the art world, but the art world does not know their game either. In a few minutes, the boy will create a disturbance and in the chaos that follows the Woman with a Doe will prise a drawing by Fernand Léger from the wall of a corridor leading to André Vidal's office. Forms all men could understand. Noble, knightly Fernand Léger.[71]

Jules and Owens are received into a cosy restaurant by an easy-mannered waiter who has saved a corner table for them. They order Martinis but go straight for mains. Jules orders roast baron of lamb, Owens goes for tenderloin with mushrooms, truffles and Madeira sauce. Owens has a notebook with him, '*He who sins against me injures himself.*'

'Old Testament.'

'Correct. *Book of Proverbs*. But it's not a game this time. I wish it was. *The perverse in heart are an abomination to the Lord.*'

At the time the two men met each other, Owens was a lubricious obsessive youth. He has developed into a socially mature professional who regards his work as distasteful but necessary. He turns his hand to that which would turn anyone else's stomach. It began with reports for daily newspapers, criminology journals, and for insurance companies seeking an unbiased opinion of a crime scene. Four years ago he narrowed his scope from those unfortunate enough to have been murdered to those unhappy enough to want to die. He became the Yard's expert on self-slaughter in the central London area.

His trips to Europe are relevant to his work not least because the subject is viewed differently in Europe than it is in Britain. Attempted suicide was decriminalised in France and most European countries after the 1789 revolution. Montesquieu thought it criminal to condemn an Englishman for trying to kill himself. He argued, quite seriously, that the English temperament is conditioned by the climate, and going crazy is a legitimate response to England's ungracious weather.[72] English law did not agree. Before 1870, suicide committed with a sound mind, once called *felo-de-se*, might have involved the forfeiture of the deceased's estate to the crown. Before 1961, if you were unlucky enough to survive an attempt, you might still have faced prosecution.

'His brain was fried, literally! A true kook! He had daubed proverbs like these on the walls of his bedsit.'

'You nicked his notebook?!'

'It's part of my work. Look at these drawings!'

'Martini white, and red, gentlemen.'

'Cheers.'

'You see? Hangings, there's the French guillotine, and the electric chair. Are they any good?'

Jules flicks through sketches of amputated bodies and twisted cadavers. 'There are few false lines. He had a clear image either before him or in his mind when he drew these. You don't suppose he was drawing them from... *from life?*'

'No one else had been in his apartment for over a year.'

'He wasn't an ambulance worker?'

'He worked half a week for a firm that sold double-paned windows. Most of his work was done on the telephone in a tiny office in Wormwood Scrubs.'

'Did he have cable television?'

'Nothing like that. He earned less than the minimum wage and lived like a tinker.'

'So he imagined it all. That makes a difference. Nearly all of them are drawn from an inferior position. Never higher than the subject. Even this one with a rope around his neck, it has been drawn from side on, from ground level, or table level. Never from above. That's unusual. How did he die?'

'He connected electrodes to his temples and ankles.'

'No sign of foul play?'

'None.'

'It's not a case of Art Brut, this guy knows what he's doing.[73] He must have taken art classes at some stage.'

'We don't have the full story. He had, in a way, erased himself from his flat. There wasn't a single document with his name on it.'

'What about these pages of notes?'

'He starts with Solomon, his love of gold, his sensuousness, his polygamy in old age… and then he's on about the judgement. You know, the story about the babies. Let's be clear about the original: Two prostitutes live together, right? Each has a son. One of the mothers wakes up with a dead baby in her arms and believes she has suffocated him in her sleep. But when she is washing the corpse for burial she becomes convinced that it is not her baby. She accuses the other mother of having substituted her dead baby for the living one and they go to Solomon. He commands that the living baby be sliced in two, and ends up giving the living baby to the woman who pleads for his life to the extent of renouncing her claim to it.'

'And which one was that?'

'The one who accused the other woman.'

'Good judgement.'

'It made Solomon the talk of the town. But my madman

figured that the mother who woke up with the dead baby in her arms really had suffocated him without knowing it. No one changed any babies. When the mother was washing the baby she couldn't accept his death. It was impossible for her to accommodate the idea that she, herself, had been the party consciously or unconsciously responsible. Driven mad with grief, she accused the other mother of having carried out the substitution, fully convinced that this was true, hoping beyond hope that her baby was still living in the arms of her companion.'

'So why did the accused woman not defend herself, if she was innocent.'

'She was a prostitute in violent times. She had no choice but to say, and these are her words in the Bible, 'I accept the king's judgement. Let the baby be neither mine nor yours, divide him.' Who *in her right mind* would oppose the king's judgement?'

'Not me.'

'And so the deluded mother, faced with the horror of 'her' child being cut in two before her eyes, pleads for his life so effectively, renouncing her own claim, that the youthful Solomon is driven to pity. He stays the soldier's sword, fully believing the grief-stricken and deluded woman to be the true mother. He gives the living baby to her.'

'The Burgundy, gentlemen.'

'Good! Very good.'

'So, the true mother is denied her own child, the crazed and desperate mother triumphs. Though her real child is dead, she believes him to be alive. Both mothers see the child they believe to be theirs grow to manhood.'

'How does that notebook end?'

'What do you think? *Proverbs* —
*Better a dish of vegetables where love is
Than a fattened ox and hatred with it.*'

The lamb and Thames Tenderloin arrive.

'Any last wishes?'

'Sorry?'

'Deranged feminine ruminator syndrome!'

'Very funny!'

'Seriously though, have you made your will?'

'Lend me that book and I'll tell you?'

'What for?'

'My new series of lectures. I'll send it back to you.'

'Fine. So?'

'So what?'

'Last wishes!'

'I want to be buried, of course.'

'Where?'

'In the same churchyard as my mother and father. I've never been adventurous. Why should I start because I am going to die!'

'Have you thought about how it will happen?'

'By accident, if today is anything to go by. That's to say, not on purpose! And not tonight, please. One scrape with death is enough for one day. What about you?'

'A silk-lined box, followed by cremation, long enough for the bones to be returned to dust. Some cremations stop before the bones have disintegrated, you know. Ashes to be distributed from Waterloo Bridge at sunset while the song plays loud. You know the one:

> *But I don't feel afraid*
> *As long as I gaze on*
> *Waterloo sunset*
> *I am in paradise!*[74]

They munch in silence, like animals, like cats, who, if you watch their ears, are afraid the slightest sound could be someone wanting to eat their dinner, or them.

'Any travel plans?'

'No plans. I'm working on another book.'

'Travel nourishes the mind, Wells!'

'It's also dangerous. Always has been. Lucas van Leyden lost his senses after visiting Zealand. Dürer died after an expedition to see a stranded whale, also in Zealand.'

'Zealand... Zealand... I came across it recently in my researches. It was Zealand that had the highest suicide rate in Europe at the end of the nineteenth century.'

'A must to avoid! Are you planning any more trips away?'

'Somewhere there are figs.'

'You like them?'

'It was on the wall of my hotel room in the Lebanon, *Where there are figs there is pleasure*.'

'I'd lay off figs and Zealand if I were you.'

'Spoken like a true insomniac!'

'Figs are riskier than you think. Fra Bartolommeo of San Marco ate too many after finishing a self-portrait and died.'

'It might have been the painting that killed him.'

'Fivizzano was killed by his own portrait of Death.'

'Was there an autopsy? Were there ever?'

'Not likely! But we know that Fra Filippo Lippi died after having a sore throat.'

'Poor fellow!'

'And Ghirlandaio after a fever.'

'That's more common!'

'Correggio shuffled off after drinking dubious well-water

while he was suffering from heat-exhaustion!'[75]

'Something approaching a diagnosis!'

'Raphael, according to legend, died of sex and Poussin would have copped it in mid-life, but he was resuscitated by the family of a chef working in Rome. He married the chef's daughter and lived to be seventy.'

'And ate well, presumably.'

'Giving the lie to Menander.'

'What's his dictum?'

'*Die young and valiantly!*'[76]

'You're quite the expert.'

'A plodder, when it comes down to it.'

'You have a good job there.'

'I was lucky. I can't teach the French a thing about art history.'

'They must have thought you could.'

'They wanted a real Anglo-Saxon!'

'And they got one! Didn't the Moderns burn out early, Bacon and Pollock and that crowd?'

'Pollock died the way he lived. Bacon lived like he was about to die. Rothko's suicide was a work of art, very carefully planned it was. Achile Gorky's was gruesome. He couldn't stand it any more. You would have hanged yourself too if you'd had his luck!'[77] But most of the big stars died old and wrinkled.'

'And the old masters, were they given to, you know, doing themselves in?'

'Elsheimer was a sad case... depressive... died in poverty. No... I can only think of de Witte. You know, cathedral interiors.'[78]

'I'm surprised there weren't more.'

'Why do you say that?'

'Because the paintings of the old masters are so often about snuffing yourself out. Don't you think martyrdom is a form of suicide?'

'Suicide is contrary to the teachings of the church.'

'But by standing their ground they generated their own punishment. Isn't that a form of suicide?'

'You're playing with words.'

'Wouldn't you agree that in provoking their tormentors to unprecedented levels of cruelty, they were purposely inciting them to sin!'

'No martyr would have provoked his tormentor to sin, or provoked his own death for that matter, for the very good reason that a person given to acting on the level of provocation would choose to save his own life if he could. The aim was not to provoke the enemy but to protect the besieged mentality, the harassed spirituality. *To resist*.'

'Though their God-given bodies be desecrated?'

'Though their intestines were unravelled before their eyes just as the pagans used to draw intestines from a living lamb. Saint Erasmus didn't choose for his intestines to be wound around a windlass.'[80]

'He must have chosen something. What did he choose, then?'

'He chose not to renounce what he believed in — his truth. That's what links painting and martyrdom!'

'Andy Warhol should do a painting of Princess Diana in the car smash. There's a martyr for you!'

'Princess Diana was not a martyr, Owens. A sacrifice, yes, but not a martyr!'

'A sacrifice then. She lives on, Wells!'

There is genuine emotion in Owens' voice.

'She is asleep, perhaps.'

'Asleep, yes. What about you? Have you managed a full night's sleep since we last met?'

Jules flinches, 'I'm pretty much over the insomnia. It's been much better lately.'

He can he tell Owens that he is more wary of sleep than ever before? How can he tell him about his dreams which seem to occur *in the spine of a second person*. He was lying on a table, and the hands of pallbearers were preparing him, smearing pigment over his skin, dark, brackish, not like blood, more like bitumen, or mud, or excrement. All he wanted was earth soft enough, firm enough to take him.

'It's nothing to be ashamed about, you know, old man. There was an article about it in *The Guardian*. Ronsard was insomniac before he died.'

'Who's talking of dying?'

'We are! He used to hear a spider running about in one of his ears and a cricket chirping all night in the other! You're in the company of geniuses!'

'I don't hear crickets!' Jules shouts, causing the conversation at the next table to halt in its tracks. The waiter picks up his notebook and heads their way.

Jules lowers his voice and leans forward, 'I hear Norma, the cellist downstairs.'

'She's beautiful?'

'Well proportioned!'

'She'll put up a good fight, then.'

'I hope so.'

The waiter is at their side, 'Gentlemen?'

They order desserts and coffee.

'The tonsure! You had me there!'

'I thought you'd like it.'

'It didn't last, you know. Later on monks were identified

by the fact that they could read.'

'So you were pardoned if you could read!'

'And strung up if you couldn't!'

'Nothing's changed. Only five per cent of the men on Death Row can read. Most of them never had a chance.'

'Condemned from birth, you might say.'

'The president can save them, can't he?'

'Yes. If he wants to play God.'

'He could probably cure people, too, if he put his mind to it. Or if the people put their minds to it. There used to be a disease, the King's Evil. The lymph glands of the neck swelled up and, strictly speaking, only medicine could have cured it. But people believed it could be cured by the royal touch. And because they believed it, it worked. Thousands were cured in France and England! It worked because they believed illness was predetermined and only the divine agent, the king, could over-ride it. Imagine living in a time like that!'

'So what's changed? Today we accept that our behaviour and character, our abilities and our likely diseases are all ghost-written in our DNA strands. How is that different from medieval pre-destination? If we believe that we are imperfect, how is that different from believing we are carriers of Original Sin or that our path is predetermined? It's goodbye to personal freedom all over again. Man has free will the way a madman in a straightjacket has it — he can choose to throw himself against the wall or onto the floor. No choice at all. The Human Genome Project is fomenting universal anxiety. Imagine, you have your genetic information scanned and discover you are carrying a gene which, in the right circumstances, will turn you green. It isn't certain you will turn green, but you tell your sexual partner and she becomes anxious. You wanted to have a child, but now you are anxious about having green children. You tell your family and in-laws about it. They are afraid that if they embrace you, they will turn green. You are stigmatised by your family. Your sexual partner becomes anxious for herself. She has read an article that the turning green gene can be transferred by making love. She is worried she might already be turning green inside. The scientists are anxious. They can't zap it. They didn't tell you before but they can't even see it to zap it! Now everybody is anxious. You have only one wish. You, the one who caused everybody so much trouble, want to die. You make arrangements. Your family and your in-laws are eager to help you. It is the least they can do. Everyone is sorry you are going to die, but they are happy that you are going to solve their problem. Just to be sure that they have not caught the green disease they get scanned as well. And each of them finds that he or she is carrying other genes, a blue gene, a yellow gene, a black gene! They have the same moral dilemma. Some keep quiet about their gene. Others do away with themselves then and there. Anxiety is everywhere. You realise that there is no need to zap yourself. It's not the green disease, it's not even the green gene, it's fear of the green gene. It's not the Plague, it's fear of the Plague.'

'Let's get out of here before we turn green, then.'

'God! Look at yourself! Too late!'

Owens has devoured his Apricots in Nightdress. Jules leaves most of his sugared halves in pastry still clothed. The platform on the other side of the metro lines is crammed full of people waiting to travel west. There is a small clearing among the crowd where a man is dancing to recorded music. The air rallies from the right. A train pulls in on the far side. There is a warning discord and the clatter of the doors closing. When it has gone the dancer is alone on the platform, perfectly still, his eternal loop continuing to play. He is staring across the lines at a woman who is standing back from a group, not as if she thinks she is above her well-dressed girlfriends, but as if she feels beneath them. The dancer decides he must speak with her. He takes his music box and lopes along to the end of the platform, flicks the

DANGER sign impudently, and descends the forbidden steps to the lines, where he proceeds to pick his way over the high-voltage cables. A girl squeezes her father's hand.

'Won't he be eleckatooted, daddy?'

Her father is also, apparently, concerned, 'Yes, sweetie. And then we'll be even later getting home to mummy.'

A current of air sweeps through the station from the left. The dancer stops half way across the tracks to turn up the volume on his machine. He makes a defiant gesture at the approaching train, which brakes abruptly. There is a bang from a fusebox somewhere. Security men run towards the dancer. A scuffle can be heard and violent cries. People are asked to be patient. The train adjusts its position with a series of violent jolts. Its doors open. Anxious passengers dismount. Anxious passengers board. The carriage is full of sweetly-smelling, if anxious, players. The air is heavy, laden with odours of birchwood and cedar, from brands such as Poison, Hypnosis and Delusion. The doors ram shut. The train judders. The lights go out and come back on. The train accelerates to speed. Lines of colour-coded wires streak past. A passenger raises her voice over the clatter of the carriage, 'I saw a man fried... in New York! On the lines! Horrible! We couldn't do anything!'

The carriage empties and a group of musicians board.

The fingers of the double bassist are like perished tyre-rubber. A woman with bloodshot eyes sings bluesily, '*I lit me a fire on yonder hill. I lit me a fire that's burning still.*'

The ride is rougher than usual. The bass player nearly loses his balance. Owens applauds them and throws them some money. A face is staring into the carriage at Jules from the bleeding lime layer. Its nose and mouth are like lobular components of some rare mountain-baboon's genitalia, frost-framed by grey mammal-bush and wisp-tailed asps of running condensation. It is Tintoretto's self-portrait, his eyes flameless, sorrowing.

A hamburger and an advanced case of dental caries enter, and voices speaking some archaic tongue. Are they not soldiers? Is it not Ancient Greek or Assyrian or Hebrew? A flash gun explodes. For the second time today Jules is stung. He puts his hand to his eyes, his cornea momentarily oxidised, the moment defined and obliterated, purged of natural colour, the world struck into grisaille. Was it not in such a flash that the infant was conceived, who would grow to be an art historian, diploma of hearsay and instructor of Parnassian prostitutes, adept in the 'nearly' tense, its verbs of regret, of historical discord, neighbourly tolerance, professional stagnancy, marital fear, and the tenseless conjugations of stalemate? Is it not in such a flash he will vanish? Owens is on his feet, haranguing the soldiers, telling them to fire their flashes in each other's eyes! Jules has Owens' arm. They burst onto ground level and enter the first club they see, baroque Parisian style, two levels. Owens gravitates to the dance floor where he sways to a hollow rhythm. Jules goes up to to the mezzanine to watch his friend in his trim suit among dancers dressed in anything but suits. He throws his head back and emits a low, hoarse appeal. The action is not one of laughter so much as a baring of the teeth, a rehearsal for the day when the skin of his lips will be eaten away. It is the laughter of the heads of Prince Egmont and Count van Hornes being eaten by birds in the year Bruegel painted *The Beggars*. It is the laughter of the skull that Arthur Gordon Pym sees in the distance grimacing from the mast of Poe's putrefying death ship.

A tango thuds in and Jules takes Owens' arm. They cut through maze-like side-streets towards The Marais. Owens is singing, slurring,

'*I wish I'd wished, I'd've wished a wish!*'

'Me too!'

'You too, Hugo?'

'A half-daft wish!'

'*I'd've wished... I'd've wished a wish-love wish.*'

'What about an enough's enough wish?'

'Swish! That's the death wish, Wells.'

'Do me a favour and have a double-expresso with me, will you?'

'Will you, won't you—?'

'Will you?'

'I will, Wells!'

They cut into a bar, where Owens throws back his coffee in quick order and calls for two whiskies crying 'Don't die on me, Dido!'

'You have to pace yourself, Owens.'

'Another bloody security eye.'

'I'm just thinking of you.'

'All these bloody security cameras. Forget it! Surveillance is a con, Wells!'

'It's a condition, that's all.'

'A new mask has been born. It hides the face behind a special horn with an eye in the end of it.'

'Do women wear the new mask?'

'Some women have bigger horns on their masks than men! But everyone ignores them. We get so used to ignoring them we become blind to them. You feel the eyes behind another horn looking at you. You stare back through the eye in the end of your horn, but neither of you notices the other's horn at all. We think we are dealing with unmasked people. It's a lie. Life is a lie that makes society tick. It makes society sick!'

Jules sneaks a look at the barman to see if he is amused or thinking of throwing them out and receives a friendly wink. Owens is warming up:

'It's like the security guard who looks at every suitcase as a bomb, every customer as a thief. We are the travellers, we are the customers who put up with it. We are accused and rifled by these seeing snouts. If we are deemed innocuous, we are deemed innocent. Everyone is accused. Everyone is observed. You don't have to be suspected to be accused. Most of us are not guilty of anything, but we merit accusation by existing. We submit to the stares of mechanical apparatuses, to interrogation. And in the control towers there are two-eyed humans with the power over human life, and they exercise it, Wells!'

He is hovering, suspended among alcoholic vapours. The barman and two customers along the bar listen intently. His eyes light up. His forehead creases. He draws breath:

'Every ruling horn has a thousand eyes feeding it information, and not one of them is rolling around in its socket, no. They practise self-control, no question. They scan the pavements in early afternoon. They scan the alleys before sun-up. They scan the airports. They scan your bedroom and they scan your dreams if you let them. They read your mail, the memory of your computer. They second-guess your intentions. They observe, they scrutinise. The eyes of time-keepers, of security guards, of witnesses and of judges are upon you at this moment and what they see is being sent to the ruling horn as we speak. The world has become an instant appraisal service, loading information into a bottomless memory, information about the growing and the decaying, the treacherous and the resilient, the helpful and the hindering. The ruling horn's mind is already made up, because it is only a mechanical eye seeing through thousands of mechanical eyes. It can't see *true* reality any more than a child can. Its information is worthless. The present has been captured, but the truth is not obvious. It claims to have captured a reality that permitted itself to be captured, that planted itself in its system. Who cares? No one. The important thing is that the false reality has been caged, the figures moving in its field of perception are appraised, accused, arrested, released, employed. You might be employed, I might be, but we still feel the eyes, thousands of eyes. We feel them as we walk along the platform, but most of all we feel them in our backs. When was the last time you walked down the street without that uncomfortable feeling? You approach a camera and you do not swerve away. Because that would be to attract attention to yourself. You walk straight ahead before the eye of the camera, allowing yourself to be captured. You do not falter under the inspection of the reading gun, the Big Eye that haunts you, views you, and reduces you to its own little criminaloid. I'm an animal! Chickens get fidgety before earthquakes. Plenty of animals have strange feelings just before a catastrophe, don't they? Answer me! Don't answer me. There are honest people around, who don't belong to the ruling horn. There is you and me and our friends here at the bar. But most people belong to the horn, even when they are in a little room where the light is low and they are staring into a mirror, into their own eyes which probe the degradation of their faces, even where there is no camera, even when their eyes tell them that death is approaching, even then their eyes belong to the horn. My eyes, our eyes, belong to us, to nature, to volcanoes and cyclones, to the coiled serpent and the breaking wave. They must not belong to Zeus or the Cyclops, not to Argus, not to governments and not to their slaves. There are assassins moving, roving, omnipresent. The ones who killed Lady Di, for example. They belong to newsreaders, to the talking heads who follow you no matter where you are in the room. They belong to the speech reading politicians, who have been trained to look up from their text *naturally*, who might as well be reading Turkish backwards, addressing no-one, doing nothing but appearing to see, to read, to address, to appear. We have been claimed by the face of advertising, whose voice addresses you in your weakest moments, whose portraits accuse you and threaten you, our eyes are not even the eyes in the photograph, the one that will remain when we have gone. We have to cut eyeholes in the one-horned masks, Wells. We have to reverse the operation of the optical authority, invert its presence. If we do not do that we are less than dead.'

The other drinkers at the bar raise a hearty 'Cheers!' and the barman offers Owens a complimentary whisky. Jules tries to soothe him. 'Everyone wants to be free, Owens. But security is necessary for society. Laws check our speed, our anger, our passions. Spontaneity is dangerous. People have to be careful. People in love, in particular.'

'People in love! People who love have to be careful! What a lie! People who love must not be careful! They must be carefree! And yet here more than anywhere, in *Le Marais*, love's playground in the City of Love, everyone agrees to be accused and suspected. Love has always been dangerous, but that doesn't mean lovers have to buy into the suspicion deal!'

They catch a south-bound taxi towards St Paul's, getting out at rue des Rosiers, where they weave haphazardly through clusters of night-people on the pavements before entering a densely-packed club whose walls are throbbing with carefully equalised frequencies.

Owens hits the dance floor where waving arms create crease marks, nightlines in a flesh-toned inferno. Jules leans on the bar, sipping a Bronx Cocktail, his face lit haphazardly by snaps of blood-red light. Above him is a widescreen video of candy men flexing glistening muscles to an inaudible soundtrack.

Now it is as if earmuffs have been lifted from his head. A voice is singing in Spanish, syllables crisp, several, distinct accompanied by banal instrumentation. He hears only English being spoken all around. Owens downs a Cloud Nine. The act alone seems to invigorate him. His voice cuts through the hammering music and insane laughter, 'Wells! Great bar! Where are we?'

'It's called Babylon!'

A low hum develops into a mystical chord as the lighting wizard bathes the dance floor in Venetian orange, then pouzzoles red and ultrmarine. As if precipitated by the turmoil, the boy who looks like St John as depicted by

Masaccio is before Jules. He tilts his head provocatively, so that the natural weakness of his face develops a menacing line from his lightly scarred forehead down an imperfect nose. He shouts in Jules' ear and points to the entrance. She is there, the Woman with a Doe. He pushes Jules in her direction. It is a nudge, and not violent, but Jules can't help thinking that it would have been enough to push him under that bus this afternoon. She has changed. She is wearing a sleeveless elastic clinging top and acrylic thigh-cut skirt, bare shaved legs lead to black-strapped demi-sandals. She is heavily made up around the eyes so they resemble those of a bird of prey. As soon as he is within reach she grabs his arm and yells in his ear, 'Have I got news for you!'

The boy gingerly lodges a cigarette between his bruised lips. Owens screws another between his own and commits the act of ignition. A dancer takes the matchbox stage, her slight figure moving like a flame. Floorlights cast her enormous vaulting shadow on the ceiling and backdrop. Frontal pin-lighting strikes her so she glitters with silver scales, a silverfish with human form, like a slave enraptured by her captivity. The music surges. Owens and the boy hit the dance floor. Jules watches the fish-like dancer before the drugged mass of dancers. His mother used to read him a story about a mermaid who died from love for a man who cut away his soul with a knife. How did it end? The decibel-level rises. A trip-hop improviser has taken the stage and is babbling to pre-recorded dance music. Owens and the boy gyrate like blitzed cockroaches as the volume takes another rise. The room darkens. Video beams shoot. Conversations are disabled. All attempts at sense have been crippled. Frequency time. Beat life. The Woman with a Doe clicks the lip of Jules' glass. In between sips they watch the sucking, shoving amoeba before them, the hypnotic dancer, or each other.

At the end of the DJ's stint the boy and Owens stumble towards the bar where Jules has a Coffee Flip for his friend, but a bean hidden in the surface of the cream sticks in his throat. He explodes in a coughing fit. The boy makes a signal to the barman who lobs an unopened bottle of Evian to him. He cuts the top off at the neck with his knife, and pulls Owens' head back by his hair, pouring the water in and over him. Owens splutters and laughs madly. The DJ is back with the dancer. The dance floor is throbbing again with bodies, the boy and Owens among them. Lights flare and strobe. Ultramarine reigns. Vivid flesh-coloured calyxes glide over the orgiasts. Now corollas appear to bloom in the space above, now paisley patterns in crimson and Van Dyck brown scale the walls.

Owens is bobbing, smoking, laughing, night-tripping, swimming with the kind of satisfaction a drowning man might exhibit on discovering he has been turned into a fish. The wide-screen is displaying a simultaneous video image of the singer on the stage. Her backing music makes use of glitches and CD skips, half-rhymes and refrains, stuttering and cries that create a new form of expression, intoxicating the throng, driving them to untutored dance phrases which they repeat like eternal sentences. The repeat impulse activates Jules and the Woman with a Doe at the bar who consume and re-order. Her eyes are bright, her mouth is glistening. He is happy. He is Mother Theresa. The boy has surely been offered a job.

Owens' arms are hanging loosely at his sides, it seems only the boy and the crowd are keeping him upright. Their faces merge in the swimming lights. The beats cut. The dancers give room. Owens does not fall. The singer's image blacks out. A DJ's voice of virgin sable fills the void as different, slower beats kick in. The new voice weaves perfectly between and within the frequencies. The Woman with a Doe is urging Jules to go. She whistles. It is a shepherd's whistle, the kind used to control dogs. The boy responds, bringing Owens with him. Her eyes are suddenly cold. Eyes of someone for whom no act is impossible. The dance floor has the anonymity of a masked ritual, an impersonal stamping horde in a breathless throe. Jules turns into the fresh night air, full of anticipation for the revelation and the intimacy that awaits him. She knows a quiet café. They turn up a side-street. She leans her head against Jules' shoulder. Their cheeks touch, and now their lips. It is a line of poetry by Louis Aragon. It is the discovery of oil painting. It is the cult of the virgin.

Finally, there is the sense that the cult of Christ is in itself a cult of virginity, not only of the Virgin Mary but of the Virgin Christ. The fired clay sculpture of Domenico of Paris, Christ and his mother, ancient and physical as the modelling mud, remind us not only of miraculous creation, not only of a virgin birth, but of a virgin death.

She draws the Léger print from her satchel.

When he comes to he is lying near a wall. He picks himself up and returns to the bar to ask the doorman if he has seen Owens or the others. He walks up and down, peering up side streets. He stares into cars. He takes the first turn right, the next left. He turns four times down narrowing lanes. Coming to a fountain, he removes his jacket and shirt, and leans over the stone edge to plunge his face into the spring water. A shock passes through him. He drives his head in and again draws it from the water, heart thumping in his throat.

He buttons his jacket over his belly. Rue des Francs Bourgeois, rue des Rosiers, rue Vieille-du-Temple, he could be on a tour of the galleries, but tonight *he* is the art exhibit. He needs to rest, a park, a square, a bush for a *giardino segreto*. Seeing a merry-go-round idle, he climbs in among the little cars and remembers:

She showed him the print and realised her mistake. She signalled to the boy who seemed to embrace Owens. Jules was about to run towards them, but suddenly he had no strength. The wrestling forms were far, too far away from him. He could not push, not one way nor the other. He fell, tasting the acid of his own stomach, hearing a cry, mad, drunk, terrified. The odour of ptomaine and urine was rising from an open culvert near his head. He tried to lift himself up. There was a pain, a second pain in his abdomen, and then blackness.

A sound is coming from his throat, a gnarled wheezing. Will his brain not explode? His skin is stretched like red lion canvas over his knuckles. What would he use to paint such a hand, powdered earth of cadmium and excrement? He would grind the pigment as he is being reduced to a few microns. His blood would be the bonding agent.

His wallet and watch are missing. The Augustine has gone. Only the madman's notebook remains. As if it will help him to find Owens, he opens it. By tilting the page towards the street lamp he finds just enough light to read:

Ovid. Metamorphosis. Snake climbs into nest, eats eight baby birds and then the mother. Calchas the soothsayer says this represents the nine years the Greeks would besiege Troy before taking it in the tenth. Homer's baby birds shriek terribly, and the mother, too. Virgil's snake is linked to the sea snakes which devour Laocoön. Prediction, fulfilment.

Book of Daniel. Daniel interprets Mene, Mene, Tekel, Upharsin: you are weighed in the balance and found wanting; your kingdom will end. True that night. King and wives and concubines drank from golden bowls taken from the temple in Jerusalem. Fault. Error. Interpretation. Judgement.

44 BC. Julius ignores soothsayer's warning and goes to his death. Disputed fault. Superstition. History, fact, myth.

Genesis XIX; i-xxvi. Lot's wife ignores warning and is turned to salt. Interdiction. Disobedience. Judgement.

Abraham's orders prefigure God's sacrifice of his son. No reason, no fault. Test of faith. Obedience.

And the following passage:

The journey is not, can not be over until the smallest has revealed its essence, until the dust has filled my mouth with its truth. Denial has followed me here, requiring a second, a third birth of me, more painful than the first which placed me at the breast of the wrong mother, who would have turned me out of myself.

A taxi approaches and he hails it though he has no way of paying. The driver will not help him. As it accelerates away, a voice says, 'Hey, man, buy some of this'. Yes, if he had money, he would buy all they had. He heads towards Owens' hotel. A chilling breeze is swooping down from the East. He hunches up, imitating a drunk, a worthless person, someone it is too late to help, someone who is too derelict to be a danger, someone to be ignored. But there is no one to ignore him. He does not hear any cars, voices or footfalls. He dares only to glance at the obedient and unlimited opacity approaching him. It is a one-word sentence like 'Fire!' No, it is the word 'River'.

He passes along thirteenth century lanes lined with twenty-first century cars. He crosses another, shorter bridge, and other night people whose language he cannot define. Owens has not checked in to his hotel. Jules explains his fears, that he might have come to some harm. The night watch sympathises, but says it is pointless to call the police before morning. Jules leaves his number. He loses one tower and another comes into view. He smells hashish and other drugs on the wind. He passes doorways where human shadows hang. He passes other dealers, other guarded doors, scouts who make quick decisions regarding who belongs here, whom to fear. They do not interrogate him. They take him for an aborigine, like themselves in the black-eyed light.

Not far from the hospital where Owens is fighting for his life, the chilled water of a Wallace fountain cuts into the dry of his throat.[80] He pushes on, gasping, drawing a double cone, he spindles, a double strand of shadow stretching and condensing from street lamp to street lamp, being born and being buried and being born again. He remembers details of the story, the one his mother read him. The fisherman stood with his back to the moon and with his knife he cut away his shadow from around his feet. The knife had a handle of green viper's skin. The mermaid's body was washed up on the shore.[82]

He can go no further.

He climbs over a locked gate into a park and drops. The landing knocks some of the wind out of him. He is like a neglected sculpture, a dusty bust in a cemetery, like that by Rodin on the grave of Castagnary.[82] A hand is near his face. He smells it before he sees it. It is lined and toughened, its pits and cracks filled with black tar. It is holding out a hand-rolled cigarette. He takes it. A lighter flashes. She lights hers first. When she offers the flame to him he all but passes out again. The trees fill with birds, chirping insanely. He gathers his strength. A faint dawn breeze. Steam is rising from a grill and drifting across the path of little stones, memory stones all of them.

He tries to stand in the eerie golden gloom. He feels overweight, top-heavy. His mouth has hit the edge of something hard. A liquid the colour of burnt carmine is running from his gums. The pain hits late. It makes him aware of another pain, not the pain in his mouth, another pain that has been there all along, as long as he can remember. Ripped by eagles, flayed by accusing warriors, revenged by treacherous lovers of indifferent gods, scratched by needle-clawed owls of the imagination, eaten from within by sharp-toothed weevils, violated by lascivious, giggling insect-devils, why is all of humanity not contorted in unpainterly agony?

The hand is fingering his mouth, pulling back the lip. A voice is telling him to spit. It is not the voice of Mélita, nor that of Teddy Moore. It is not the hand nor the voice of the Woman with a Doe. *Then shall I know even as also I am known.*[83] He hears Owens and the boy struggling, falling. Is it love or death? The Woman with a Doe goes to Owens. She turns him on his side. A pool gathers about the gash.

Jules opens his mouth. He would roar full-throated. He would say No-oh-oh! like a jungle animal, like a hippopotamus in a drought, one that has had enough of carrying its cumbrous bloated form from cadaver to cadaver, as if this might prevent Owens' life from ebbing away.

The hand is slapping him. That voice, again, the one with the cigarette, is telling him to be quiet. It is saying they have to go. It is speaking to another. They prop him up. The woman lights a cigarette for her friend. An image of eight bearer ants disappears into the lighter flash, incinerated by the hundred-fold gesture. They are shaking him. Everybody has to get out. The cops come round at 6 o'clock. Anyone inside will be taken away for a hose-down.

He falls a third time. He asks, 'Is there more than one way out?' The image returns, of ants. Will he be carried back to the heart of the nest in the jaws of the bearers? He balances. An automatically timed sprinkler comes into play. The light splits into a rainbow in the haze. He strokes a curve in the air, as if it is the furry back of an arched animal, or a huge cerebral nerve. They call to him to follow. They return and help him. He strives to be conscious. Their feet are scraping the gravel path. He says, 'I'm not one of you. I've been robbed. I have friends.'

'Hey! You hear that, Jacques? He's got friends!'

Jacques is the kind of guy who is not easily amused. He replies coldly, without looking at Jules, 'We've all got friends, pal. We've all been robbed.'

The first rays of sunshine pass between buildings as they make for the broken gate. Jules knows if he does not remain upright he will fall into the lap of his phantoms like a baby, to die of distemper pouting for a nipple. He has to stand. He has to take his first steps. He is between his parents, his new parents, ones who have no real choices though they have chosen to help him.

He is driven by one thought, to make it to his apartment. It will be as if nothing has happened. The cleaning trucks will roll by. Norma will begin to play. The phone will ring.

He begins the journey, through the tunnel of gravid shade, homewards, by means tortuous, peristaltic, swallowing images before and expelling them behind, each image possessing its own intoxicating fluidity, event without moment, presence without mass filling, packing his cortex tighter and tighter, which beats like a cardiac pod, and releases him into the subsequent street, the consequent seconds.

Let it follow, let it flow. Infancy, superstition, borrowage and bluster, song, prayer and poem. Frames break in succession, a tide is drawing up over him. And so cold. No, he is not on a shore. He is an age over which some inconceivable ice-cap is thickening.

Now he has stopped. Suspended. Empty. The emptiness has penetrated him. There is no colour scale. The world reasserts itself, fatuous, flirtatious, insipid. He is between two universes, one where the disinherited choose to help you and the other one, where you order, you drink your coffee and you pay for it. A waiter has just finished setting up tables on a footpath. Jules picks a cube of sugar from a bowl and keeps walking. *The hermits knew they would sin if they entered the city.*

Such a chance we have been given to feel, to understand. Yet we inflict imitation upon our children, as if replication were possible. We praise our professors, doctors, captains — for what? For their sleight of hand? Where is he whose weapon can gainsay the wound? We are of those whose light is an extension of night, whose sound issues from the workshop of the volcano, whose fruit is the outcome of rotting, whose affirmation is the result of a denial. We are of those neither hot nor cold, forever-going-between, or, worse, we are inert, those who know no narrative, clinging to possessions, who purchase, plan-patent, code-deciphered. We are of those who meet the conditions, who observe meaningless festivals, who dishonour the artists and harvest scant knowledge, whose marker does not shift, it is the costume of earthly law.

Tears understand. According to the scientists, they heal, or have antiseptic qualities. They are the onomatopoeia of painters. Rogier van der Weyden caught them. Hans Holbein the Elder learned from them. They remind us we are seconds after the beginning of life's ending. The geode revolves. Rocks orbit rocks. We draw circles because we must. We never grow tired of them. A circle is greater than we are. There are some paintings, some poems that can never be heard too often, because they, too, are greater than we are. A line compasses the universe. Flames eat their circles outwards. The world ends in a conflagration, and, with it, Not Knowing will end.

And knowing? Will knowing remain, orbiting? Do you know? Can you know? Knowing will complete the circle. Knowing will capture another revolution. Yes, it has been proven. The future will be darker. There will be, will be... fewer stars. A cold dark place, sunless, deathless. Sky without stars and life eternal, emptier by the year, time without end and meaningless. And those flowers of nature... of science, of ignorance... are no more... rocks orbiting rocks... omniscient. Far, his unknown companions of the park. Returned to the night, his guardians.

He enters a smoky café that has been open all night. Some of the clientele look as though they have been there for quite some time, they have that jaded look about them. Another group appears to have recently risen and showered. They have arranged themselves according to gender, men at one locus, women at the other. Are we in the twenty first century, or experiencing the remains of the fifteenth, or in a museum at night, witnessing the coming-to-life of the linden sculptures of Daniel Mauch, varnished flesh bulging at the knots, flowing, pigmented, powdered?[84] What language is that, medieval, rural? What pharmacist coloured those merlot lips? What god, whom they will never find, are they seeking? Jules takes a table near a poker machine.

'What's it to be?'

The waiter has been on his feet for six hours. The lights above cast the shadow of his nose down over his chin. He leans towards Jules and detects traces of alcohol. He hopes Jules still has some money. Morning light floods the bar, shoving the shadow of the barman's nose clean off his face.

'Just a cup of coffee, thanks.'

Jules measures the distance he will have to cover to make good his escape. Does visibility exist apart from the objects perceived? No information. Impossible to verify. Even when true at time of visibility. In retrospect, regarding birth, intensity, mood and tendency, all is unclaimable. We can only accomplish inaccurate reconstitution.

To do mountains in fresco or secco, make a verdaccio colour, one part black, the two parts of ochre. Step up the colours, for fresco, with lime-white and without tempera; and for secco with white lead and with tempera. And apply to them the same system of shadow and relief that you apply to a figure.[25]

The coffee arrives. We are raised against gravity, and all the world on the air side of the birdless dark is ours. Paradise pasture-sure. He just has to get through that doorframe. He has fused the subjective and the objective at the level of the cardinal sign. He has raised the cup and emptied its contents. He has tasted something resembling coffee, something resembling sugar. A fatigued barman wants payment. The wave breaks on the new chiliad, ever breaking, ever a new age. We have passed by the seven combinations of the order of importance of Art Philosophy and Religion and arrived at the eighth, $. Euro. Small change. Have none. He glances at the bar. A huge convex mirror is positioned above the wash-room staircase. Is it any wonder many artists drew disks such as lenses, distorting glasses and concave mirrors, which gave a distorted picture of the world about, world in which there was no painter, no parent. They knew the anonymity of the bomb. The bang. The birth of the work. Like spring. Van Eyck did not make afresh but forced light through the filter of his applications. Lenses gather and divert, or concentrate. We see circles, those rings around candles, rainbow hazes, parasalene moons. Do they startle other life forms, birds, plants? Are we alone in being able to contemplate existence?

Now, he could draw, now, to divert the waiter's attention. He asks a neighbour for a pencil and gets a biro. The sun elides between clouds, bursting out and dimming by turns. He has the feeling of having found what he was looking for, but a tension entering, re-entering his tendons pushes this sense of discovery into the memory. His stomach squizzles. He has drawn the café interior on an envelope, the windows and, above all, the door frame. The waiter goes into the kitchen and Jules walks through the door he has been drawing. No cries follow him, but the morning shouts of a shopping precinct reach him. As he leaves a pedestrian mall the sun catches him with all its force, an eight thousand wide kilometre band of illumination that nearly blinds him.

Thighs chafing against the weave, he hears the sound of a shop's metal-blind being raised. A bakery. Only it is not his baker. Not home yet. He passes dozens of buildings, extraordinary in themselves, but nondescript because they lack associations for him. He crosses before hundreds of impatient, idling cars. He stumbles upon a familiar corner. A public commission. Rejected. An unwanted sculpture. Dreyfus, defaced with yellow paint: 'Sale traître.'[85]

Boulevard du Montparnasse. Boulevard Port Royal. The maternity hospital. A cold tongue-taste of some metallic salt. His mouth waters warm as blood. He turns like a blind man in a familiar space, registering the familiar scuffle of business, the punctuality of deliveries, the sounds, their quality, the acoustic of his quarter. The eyelash moon fades as it slides into the view of other insomniacs in other hemispheres. He sees a drift of light, blue in a volume of air above the concealed river, and, further off, above one of the gardens, a shifting luminescence, now hard like a cut silhouette, now plasmatic, pulsing like the ganglion of a primitive life-form.

Too late! His baker has seen him. Jules aims directly for the giant doors that shield the courtyard within from the street. He rests his head against his fist, numbers reeling through his mind. He punches a code. Wrong. Again wrong. The door clicks, it is the customs inspector from the third floor leaving for work. He does not wish the professor Good morning. He makes as if he has not seen Jules at all. He holds the door open as he might do for a complete stranger and Jules slips in. The customs officer shakes his head in the direction of the baker, who raises his brows and grimaces. A man should know his limits at Jules' age.

The lift rises up the spigot of the spiral stairs. Did he press button A? The lift is speaking, only the voice is garbled. It is not speaking French. It is incomprehensible in any language, tangled, mangled, a recording that has been unplayed for too long. Jules' ears are filled with the syllables of a lost language, a pre-language of advanced if bewildered primates. He approaches his door.

A note from Norma is wedged into the frame. 'Tickets, yes! Excellent seats. See you tomorrow. 11am?' Tomorrow is today. How much time does a man need to put his shop in order? As his key enters the lock, he hears them inside, shuffling guiltily to their positions like children behind a curtain.

Four at floor level and four in the upper corners, each is occupied with some task under his cagoule. They sing:

> *The red petticoat under the flashing arches*
> *has recovered its price twenty times over*
> *another voyage is effaced*
> *from another city's memory.*
>
>> *Where is our lord?*
>> *Hidden in the stolen mirror?*
>
> *Gentle the one who returns*
> *for whom does he reach?*
> *For the unknown girl fingering Petrarch?*
>
>> *Mother, where are you?*

We are the tendrils
rootcut
hands disembodied
given life by phrase.

We eschape the sign
ensample inscribed
as richly he went to his execution
we row upon his absence.

Where, but where, the flowerhead?

For no place but this and longing
our clothe was cleansed.
Give our melodies leave
ever overleft.
We are many and wanting
fasted, hungering.

Who will repeat our refrain?
Who interpret?
Who give-cradle?
Passing he saw and held us.

He knows us and his knowledge forthwith
outsays his silence
a mode shaping alike and again
we are his attributes and his shortcoming.

The voice of the crier
and of his children
we are his best
his only.

Hear us, oh hear us, songwinds!

Jules raises his hand. Eight stunted reminders of the boy Jules who accompanied his father to Paris in 1962 fall silent. His answer machine is blinking but there is no message, only the sound of someone hanging up, two, three times. Is it the hotel or the police or the woman and the boy? Will they offer to ransom Owens' life? He phones the police. They have no record of any incident involving Owens. He wills Owens to be alive, to be well. He wills him into the Book of Life. His clothes fall from him. Not exactly Adam. The skin over his empty belly is like a battlefield of flattened hairs. He smears liquid soap over his body and stands shivering in the shower waiting for the water to warm up. It does not. He steps under the jets. The blast of cold water nearly stops his heart. With a towel around his shoulders, his skin a field of goose-bumps, he raises each tool in turn: electric razor, mouthwash, hair-oil.

The pleurants in heavy cowls and cassocks, the truants so like his brothers, sprung from the same seed, scuttle from their corners to the centre of the room, each carrying a particular object. There is the Pompeiian lamp. Knotted fingers have his whalebone pipe, his laser pointer, the bottle of sleeping tablets. There are a few of his better life drawings; the Lucas van Leyden print, *The Plague in Holland*. One is holding the note from Norma. Arriving at the table, bare except for its centrepiece of stale croissants, each places his object before him and plays with it awkwardly, spilling the oil, the tobacco, removing batteries from the laser pointer, spreading out the two-toned pills, smudging the charcoal of the drawings. The last holds Norma's note to his breast, looks at it at arm's length and holds it again to his breast.

Jules goes to his bookshelves, takes a book and reads aloud,

>*Quid terras alio calentis*
>*sole mutamus patriae? Quis exsul*
>*se quoque fugit?*[86]

Has an exile ever fled from himself? They lower their heads. Their true possessions, their lord's demesne, memory of their fields, their century, their sepulchral selves await them.

He takes a wear-shiny suit and pulls it over his shivering hide. He opens the door and they all descend the circling stairs. He swings the massive portal open. The handle feels small in his hand, his fist appears grand and muscled like that of a Rubens god. He walks at his usual pace, with his usual gait, not bending forward nor overly upright, slightly flat-footed, never looking back. They are behind him, inflecting,

> *Day eight.*
> *The words of the Annunciation*
> *have born fruit.*
> *The seed is rising.*[87]

They cross the Garden of Marco Polo under the shade of awakening branches, their nosing buds. We catch sight of ink-black vestments passing a semi-circular pantheon of parchment-toned goddesses. They advance down wide steps bordered by new seasons flowers in full bloom, entering the perspective of the Luxembourg Gardens, 'comme en Paradis', as de Musset described it. They skirt the octagonal basin that spreads before the Florentine palace, their forms reflected in undulating black waters, the false declivity of the pond of the Fountain of the Medicis, where Polyphemus leans menacingly over the ignorant lovers. Galatea admires stretched-out Acis. Two river-gods, one of them prefiguring Blake's Nebuchadnezzar, pour their still waters over the scene of joy and misery, compatibility and repulsion, love and jealousy.

> *Abiding be his passion*
> *his stem of sorrow veined with emerald!*
> *Lemon blossom rain*
> *from the stamens of Sidon!*

> *Weep ye daughters!*

> *Dust cover us*
> *we are chaste with strife of the birth-year.*
> *Venus be born!*
> *A father's offcuts merge with the foam*
> *his blood and sperm crested*
> *on the shore of unanswering land!*

Where, oh where, is our lord?

*We will endure longer nights with him
laid under stone which never warms.
Shall attend him
serving the will
of anonymous tongues.
Without argument
his gallants in sweat-life
maidens in grave-sleep.
Ours are not the love-man's appurtenances
nor his strongroom of lust-objects.*

Hear us, oh songwinds!

Obedient to traffic signals they pass the Odéon Theatre alive with students, actors seeking work, the inevitable beggars, all written into the books of life of others. Architects and businesswomen ignore Jules and his choristers on boulevard St Germain. The new seasons fashions have caught on, they do not have eyes for heavy capes, they were all the rage last year. Jules stops the procession for a moment by the Abbey of St Germain, not to pay homage to the ancient scribes, but to honour the return of a bronze bust l'Hommage à Apollinaire, once again visible.[88] He intones Picabia's 'Art is visible, like God,' and the pleurants keen the words after him. He cries, 'Art is a pharmaceutical product for imbeciles!' and the Eight keen accordingly.[89]

They file before boutiques packed with African sculptures, Sri Lankan masks, ancient maps, nineteenth century portraits, miniature master works believed lost, undetected forgeries, medieval sacred objects and Sumerian clay tablets. There is hardly enough room for Jules and the Eight on the narrow footpath of rue Bonaparte. The light strengthens — the river is near.

Quai Malaquais, 'mal acquis', is wide, their train is long, their step is even, slow, slower than that of others on the pedestrian crossing who are already stepping up onto the footpath opposite. The signal changes, illuminating a warning in red. Will they make it? A hundred diesel trucks, chauffeur-driven limousines, electric cars and gas-powered buses are revving, impatient for the green light. An observer in the control brain of Paris-central holds her breath as a man in a worn-out suit appears to have lost his sense of direction in the middle of the street. He is gesturing wildly, as if herding a group of schoolchildren. But she can not see any children. She can not see the Eight. Jules steps off the road, the screws of the anxious motors turn, the traffic races.

They define Pont des Arts, toes peeping out regularly from under their cloaks. They pass before beggars wasting away in the wind, who, though have the gift of insight, are incurable. One is clutching his stomach. Not the magic potions of the Indies, not mercury, not China root, not sarsaparilla can cure him. Another offers a tooth, which he has carried in his hand for two days, in return for a cure for his *Sweatyng Sicknesse*. He throws it at Jules. It passes over his head and plips into the Seine. Their time on the bridge will be brief. Neither Jules nor the Eight have the power to heal, not the voiding wounds of the interior, the diseases of poverty, not the misdemeanours of the secret places, the bitter rewards of *luxuria*, nor the graceless sins of the bourgeoisie. Theirs is not the holy wood. On the quai du Louvre the Eight turn left as one to commit their last choreography.

At the points of an octagonal fountain in the Jardin des Tuileries, they raise their right arms as one, and make a sweeping gesture before their robes as if beheading the last wheat stems of the harvest. They resemble neunes signalling in time the integrality of their return to medieval parchment, accepting the punishment of God, *flagitium Dei*. Where, oh where, is their lord?

Where surveillance has no end
where he is well-appointed
by the scribe of the catalogue.

We the apprenticed in death
desire investiture.

Grant it us, oh take us, seigneur!

Jules claps his hands and without hesitating they enter the museum. Their nights will be peopled by night-watchmen carrying torches, by day they will suffer the indignities that go with their term. Slowly, deliberately, they take up their positions, faces obscured, around the effigy whose face is seeking its proper shape. As if it is being worked by invisible fingers, now it resembles the face of knightly Teddy Moore, now that of the late Mr Wells, now Owens, whose eyes stir under his closed lids. He comes to in the emergency theatre. A doctor, astonished, issues urgent instructions as the face of the gisant settles on that of Philippe Pot, High Bailiff of Burgundy, commander of the sepulchre. The living have escaped from the dead.

When Jules steps outside the museum it is as if a lid, some gigantic disc or a menacing mass such as a suspended rock, has been lifted from over the Paris basin. The surgeon has finished his work and he sees, like Bartimaeus, sight restored.[90]

There are the shining gates of the Luxembourg Gardens.
The red marble of the optician's entrance.
There is Norma entering the bakery.

And I saw a new heaven and a new earth.[91]

Paris, 1998–2003

NOTES

1. From *Bodily Presence*, by W.H.Oliver and Anne Munz. Poems and colour reproductions of original oil paintings. Blackberry Press, Wellington. 1993.

2. Many families chose to move to France rather than adopt Algerian nationality when Algeria gained its independence on July 3 1962. They became known as 'pieds-noir rapatriés (en France)', or 'black-feet returned (to France)'.

3. *The Card Players*, Pieter de Hooch (1629–1684). Completed c.1663–65. Bought by the Louvre 1801 for 1,350 francs. 65 x 77cm. Some adults entertain themselves at cards and flirtation as a boy waits, jug in hand, to serve them wine. It is possible, if not highly probable, that Jannetge van de Burgh and one of de Hooch's children were the models or inspirations for these personalities and others like them in other paintings. De Hooch married de Burgh in 1654, their seventh child was born in 1672, at least two of their children died in infancy (from church records). They were buried

in 1663 and 1665, the years of creation of *The Card Players*, when their oldest child would have been around eight years old. De Hooch is known to have used a pin (with a string attached) inserted at the vanishing point to formulate his lines of perspective. He was reduced to penury during his life and appears to have died in an asylum.

4. *Jupiter and Antiope*, Hendrick Goltzius (Mühlbrecht 1558–Haarlem 1617) 100 x 133cm. Louvre. Gift of the Baron Basile de Schlichting 1914. Antiope appears to be in a sensual trance. Her stillness and bliss contrast with the agitation and mischievous thirst of Zeus, whose very beard seems to be aroused. Antiope's breasts shine as if they are tender, perhaps from feeding, and are certainly charged with milk. The nipple of the left one is 'looking' directly at the viewer, the right one is letting fly a fountain of four fine jets. In mythology, Antiope became, by Zeus, the mother of twins. Later, she was driven mad by Dionysus and wandered through Greece in a deranged state till she was cured by Phocus, the grandson of Sisyphus, who married her.

5. From *Acis and Galatea,* by John Gay, (1685–1732)

> *O ruddier than the cherry!*
> *O sweeter than the berry!*
> > *O nymph more bright*
> > *Than moonshine night*
> *Like kidlings blithe and merry!*

6. Andy Warhol (1928–1987) entered New York City hospital for a routine gall bladder operation. Following complications he died on the 22nd February, dubbed 'a day of medical infamy' by

one biographer.

7. The story of Polyphemus the Cyclops' love for Galatea ends badly: Polyphemus surprised Galatea with her lover Acis, a beautiful shepherd boy of Sicily (and son of Pan). Taking a huge rock, he crushed Acis to pieces. Acis's blood, gushing from under the rock, was changed by Galatea into the river Acis, now *Fiume de Jaci*, at the foot of Mount Etna. There is a representation of Polyphemus spying on the lovers from behind a rock, in the secluded Medici Fountain, Luxembourg Gardens.

8. *Enterrement à Ornans,* Gustav Courbet (1819–1877). Musée Orsay. Painted 1849–1850. Gift of Mlle Juliette Courbet, 1881. Louvre, 1882. Transferred to Orsay, 1986. 3.15 x 6.68M. An altar boy holding an incense burner, his face painted with fresh rose tones and his eyes full of vitality, seems mentally removed from the scene of the burial, where all levels of the village population are represented in various states of mourning. Ornans was the artist's birth place (Franche-Comté). Courbet fought hard to be accepted by the Paris salons that had rejected his work. By the 1860's he was exhibiting regularly, recognized as the chief representative of the French realist movement. An ardent revolutionary and humanist, he was involved in the Paris Commune, and even held an administrative position in the interim organisation of 1871. After the Commune was overthrown, his signature was discovered on a document authorising the toppling of the Trajan–column-like column in Place Vendôme, a symbol of Napoleonic imperialism and of burgeoning capitalist tendencies. He was sentenced to six months in prison and ordered to pay an impossible

fine for its re-erection. He died in exile in La Tour de Peilz, Lake Geneva, Switzerland, December 31, 1877. He was 58.

9. Hogarth, William (London, 1697–1764, London). From the mid 1730s through the 1750s he produced many paintings and prints—satirical moral progresses (*The Harlot's Progress*, *Marriage à la Mode*, *The Four Stages of Cruelty*). Their success inspired pirated copies, inciting him to campaign for the passage of the Copyright Act of 1735. Notably xenophobic, Hogarth advocated a national English school of art, freed from the traditions of the Continental schools. In 1753, he published *The Analysis of Beauty*, a home-spun theory of aesthetics supported by his own examples. In it he speaks about what was later to be called physiognomy as indicative of mental soundness or ability: 'It is strange that nature hath afforded us so many lines and shapes to indicate the deficiencies and blemishes of the mind, whilst there are none at all that point out the perfections of it beyond the appearance of common sense and placidity.... All that the ancient sculptors could do, notwithstanding their enthusiastic endeavours to raise the characters of their deities to aspects of sagacity above human, was to give them features of beauty.'

10. *The Criminal Man,* Lombroso, Cesare (Verona, 1835–1909, Turin). Published, 1875. Lombroso held that criminals exhibit mental and physical anomalies due to degeneration and to atavism (reversion to a primitive evolutionary stage). He believed criminal types could be identified by their physical characteristics. His ideas were disputed by Charles Goring and many others. During his life he did much to improve conditions for prisoners.

11. Before Kretschmer and Lombroso, Physiognomy's champion and founder was Johann Caspar Lavater (Zurich, 1741–1801, Zurich). His ideas had an ineradicable effect upon European thinking for two hundred years. The stir he caused at the time can be felt in the following extract from *Tableau de Paris* by dramatist and politician Louis-Sébastien Mercier (Paris, 1740–1814, Paris). The book from which the extract is taken was discovered without cover or title page in a discarded box outside a boarded-up bookshop, rue du Poteau, Paris, Wed, 19th February, 2003. The typography has been slightly modernised. The text, it turned out, was published in Amsterdam, 1783 as *Tableau de Paris* (1781–1789). "O que M. Lavater, docteur Zuricois, qui a tant écrit sur la science de la physionomie, n'est-il au Palais - Royal le vendredi, pour lire sur les visages tout ce qu'on cache dans l'abyme des cœurs!

"Il verroit, je crois, que l'habitant de Paris, n'est ni cruel, ni farouche, ni porté à la révolte; mais n'y découvriroit-il pas un mélange d'astuce, de finesse, de présomption, de suffisance et de *hauteur*? Il n'est pas né pour des sentiments extrêmes; et il a beau aspirer à l'extrême licence des mœurs, il n'y parviendra même pas....[M]ais voici ce que je pense sur la physionomie.

"Les bonnes qualités du cœur impriment toujours à la physionomie un caractère touchant. Jamais un excellent homme n'a paru d'une figure désagréable; l'humanité empreint sur les traits du visage une sorte de sérénité & de douceur.... Ce sont les inclinations basses & mauvaises, qui font toutes ces figures révoltantes & mesquines; la beauté est moins un don de la nature qu'un attribut secret de l'âme & de ses dispositions habituelles. Un homme sensible se reconnoît à ses attitudes, à ses regards, à sa voix. Couvrez son visage de cicatrices, coupez-lui un bras; ni l'œil ni l'accent n'auront perdu leur expression.

"Il est presqu'impossible de dissimuler l'envie, la malice, la cruauté, l'avarice, la colère; et les passions généreuses ou viles ont des nuances qui se révèlent à l'œil attentif." Chapter CLXII, 'Palais-Royal', in Volume II, pp 173–176. ('If only Mr Lavater, the Zurich doctor who has written so much about the science of physiognomy, were at the Palais-Royal on Fridays, to read on the faces all that is hidden in the deepest recesses of the heart. He would see, I believe, that the inhabitant of Paris is neither cruel nor wild, nor given to revolt. Would he not rather discover there a mixture of astuteness, of finesse, of presumption, of self-importance, and of loftiness? He (or she) is not born for extremes of sentiment, and though s/he appears to aspire to an extreme liberty of behaviour, s/he will not achieve it. ...[B]ut here is what I think about physiognomy. The good qualities of the heart always give an endearing aspect to the physiognomy. Never has an excellent man cut a disagreeable figure. Humanity lends the traits of the face a sort of serenity and mildness.... Base and evil tendencies make all faces revolting and mean. Beauty is less a gift of nature than a secret attribute of the soul and of its habitual dispositions. A sensitive man can be recognized by his attitude, his looks and his voice. Cover his face with scars, cut off an arm, and neither his eye nor his accent will have lost their expression. It is well-nigh impossible to conceal envy, malice, cruelty or anger; while generous or vile passions have nuances which reveal themselves to the attentive eye.')

Regarding Lavater, see *Physiognomische Fragmente zur Beförderung der Menschenkenntnis und Menschenliebe* (4 vol., 1775–78; English translation, *Essays on Physiognomy*, 1789–98; French translation, *Fragments physiognomoniques*, 1774–1778). Lavater began by searching for traces of the divine in the visible world, and was led to considering the face as manifestation of the spirit. His research develops the Aristotelian (behaviour and appearance are related) theories of Giambattista Della Porta (*De Caelesti physiognomonia*, 1601) in which the features are linked to one of four categories of character: phlegmatic, choleric, sanguine and melancholic. Lavater also initiated researches into the link between handwriting and personality, later known as graphology. F.J.Gall's (1758–1828) theories of phrenology then became fashionable. Gall suggested that the mental faculties and character traits were brought about in large part by the shape of the skull and the brain, and specific areas of the brain were responsible for specific functions. This was disproved in 1824 by M. Flourens, who showed that different parts of the brain had an *action commune*, as well as a less significant *action propre*, in other words it was not possible that the shape of the head (or the face, or the body) predetermined health or intelligence or behaviour. However, certain motor and sensory function centres in the brain were; in fact, located not long after, with the result that, although Physiognomy as a science is now regarded as a charlatan practice (a horrific and dangerous one in the hands of the Nazis), certain *physiognomic signs* do have definite correlatives in psychological function or malfunction.

12. Denis Diderot makes his claim about the good grace of the

populace in *Jacques the Fatalist* using the 'voice' of the author, though he later tells us this is one of Jacques' notions. Written 1755–1784.

13. Botticelli, *Virgin and Child*. Distemper on poplar. 89.4 x 56.5cm. Fogg Art Museum, Harvard University, Boston. Given to museum by Grenville L. Winthrop who had bought it from a dealer in New York in 1923.

14. *De Gave Gods: De Pest in Holland vanaf de late Middeleeuwen*, 1988. Leo Noordegraaf and Gerrit Valk.

15. Pliny the Elder (AD23/4–79), Roman naturalist, soldier and friend of Emperor Vespasian. One surviving work, a thirty seven volume encyclopaedia of natural science.

16. 'Customs of the Roman Empire' in *Valerius Maximus* (parchment, 306 pages, 55 x 38 cm, 86 miniatures plus text and margin decorations). Bibliothèque Nationale, Paris (Folio 51 of manuscript 6185). Valerius Maximus lived at the beginning of the first century AD, in the reign of Tiberius. The text was translated (c. 1442) by Simon de Hesdin and Nicolas de Gonesse. The pages were painted by unknown artists although specialists have identified the same hand in different miniatures. The book was created at a time when Burgundian miniaturism was developing out of its primitive phase, giving more humanity to its figures, more volume to its forms, greater depth to its perspective, while its painters were gaining control in both the formal and technical use of pigments. The word 'miniature' derives from *minium*, the brilliant red pigment once used by a rubricator, (the artisan who inscribed titles and first lines). The word was adopted to refer to the paint-

ings that evolved out of frame, border, and elaborate initial. The word 'illumination' derives from the fact that early gold or, more rarely, silver embellishments gave the impression that pages had, literally, been illuminated. The scene is the last stage of a banquet. There is music and restrained revelry. Some guests have departed, some couples are embracing in an unrestrained manner. A cleric looks on disparagingly. The figures are depicted in 13th century clothing.

17. Ms Lat. N° 17 d'Evreux. Page of musical notation from F° 11, for two voices, containing eighteen musical cells (types of variable bars), dated 1262. The sung prayer is: *Spiritus et alme orphanorum paraclite primogenitus Marie virginis matris ad Marie gloriam Mariam sanctificans Mariam gubernans Mariam coronans.* Contained in 'Problèmes de notation musicale. (Notations médiévales des manuscrits d'Evreux)' by A. Machabey in *Annales Universitatis Saraviensis VI*, 1957. The piece of music was written for monks stationed in Wareham, now a municipal borough in South Dorset situated between the Frome and the Piddle Rivers in England. The monks there were dependent upon the Benedictines of the Lyre Abbey of the Diocese of Evreux (100 km W.N.W. of Paris).

18. *Daphnis et Chloë* 2nd Suite (composed 1909–12), Maurice Ravel (Ciboure 1875–Paris 1937). Ravel adapted two orchestral suites from the ballet score composed for Diaghilev, choreographed by Fokine, and first performed 1912 by the Ballet Russe whose dancers included Karavina and Nijinsky. The story is taken from a 3rd century BC pastoral romance by the Lesbian Longus. Ravel developed the potential of the orchestra by empowering its

different parts (subdivisions of subdivisions). He made use of sound painting, especially by means of a gently sustained wordless vocal chorus.

19. *The Night Watch* (or *The Company of Captain Frans Banning Cocq and Lieutenant Willem van Ruytenburch* — known by other titles besides). Rembrandt van Rijn (Leyden, 1606–69, Amsterdam). Canvas. 363 x 437cm. 1642. On loan from City of Amsterdam since 1808. Rijksmuseum, Amsterdam. The first title was given to the painting by art critics at the beginning of the 19th century. However, restoration after the 2nd World War showed that it was not a night scene at all. *La Ronde de Jour* (Day Watch) was suggested. It has, with time, lost personages and its original dimensions. Individuals, pairs and groups are depicted, each materially preoccupied. Only a young girl seems uninvolved in the machinations of the adult world. Golden tones emanate from her, she seems to shine with her own light.

20. *The Original Sin*, Lucas van Leyden (1489–1530, Leyden). Copper plate engraving. 1529. 7.2 x 11.5cm. Rijksmuseum, Amsterdam.

21. *Adam and Eve*, Albrecht Dürer (1471–1528, Nuremburg). Engraving, 1504. Collection Dutuit, Musée du Petit Palais, Paris (also London British Museum). Eve is receiving an apple from the snake while concealing another in her left hand. Willem Vrelant, *Book of Hours*, illuminated MS circa 1460. 'The Original Sin'. Ludwig IX 8, fol. 137r. Malibu. J. Paul Getty Museum. The devil here has a woman's face, hair and manner of curling around the tree-trunk! The engraving in which Adam is holding out two

apples is by Marcantonio Raimondo, *Adam and Eve* (after Raphael). 23.9 x 17.6cm. Print Room, British Museum. Marcantonio suffered humiliation for completing a series of erotic engravings. He also suffered debt, for political reasons, and retired to obscurity. Mantegna (1431–1506) includes a small representation of Adam and Eve at the bottom of *La Vierge de la Victoire* (1496, Louvre) in which the snake's head resembles a sunflower while Adam and Eve both possess the fruit of knowledge of good and evil and a third apple is millimetres from Adam's left hand.

22. *Cripple healed by the shadow of St Peter,* Tommaso di Giovanni di Simone Guidi, known as Masaccio (1401, San Giovanni Valdarno–1428, Rome). 232 x 162cm. Painted 1425–26. Based on an episode related in Acts of the Apostles V, 12–14. The Brancacci Chapel (unfinished 1425–28), situated to the right of the transept of the Santa Maria del Carmine, Florence, was dedicated to the Madonna of the People. Fresco. Masaccio was so devoted to art that 'he refused to give any time to worldly causes, even to the way he dressed' (Vasari). The apostle John, next to St Peter is believed to be a self-portrait.

23. Advertising hoarding depicting *Mon Seul Désir*, the largest of six tapestries (3.12 x 3.30M) known as *The Lady and the Unicorn* (*La Dame à la licorne*). See Note 62.

24. *The Beggars (*also known as *The Cripples)*, Peter Bruegel the Elder (Brögel, Northern Brabant, c.1525–1569, Brussels). Painted in 1568. One of his last works. Wood panel, rare at the time. His smallest surviving work. 18 x 21 cm. Coincidentally, 21 year old Miguel Cervantes was in the Brussels Grand'Place in 1568 where

he witnessed the grisly execution of Egmont, Prince of Gavre and of the Grand-Admiral Philip of Monmorency, Count van Hornes. Their heads were displayed on pikes by order of the king of Spain. In 1566, the presentation of a petition to Margaret of Parma in Brussels by four hundred young confederates, all of them sons of nobility, was dubbed the Beggars' Rebellion after a comment made by the Count of Berlaymont, 'afraid of those beggars ?' (in French, *gueux*). Their cry of their rebellion became, '*Vivent les Gueux!*'. The rebellion was a significant event preceding the executions mentioned above, and the extermination of between fifty thousand and a hundred thousand suspects and opponents to the Spanish-controlled regime (reports of the massacres vary). Gift of Paul Mantz, 1892. Louvre.

25. *Trattato della Pittura*, Leonardo da Vinci (Vinci, Tuscany 1452–1519, Cloux, France). Codice Vaticano Urbinate 1270. Leonardo observed nature closely, trying to understand its irregularity, changes in humidity, in temperature and the tiny shifts in atmospheric pressure contributing to unseen currents of air which define each day from all others. (eg §787. *Perchè i monti in lunga distanzia si dimostrano più scuri nella cima che nella base*. 'Mountains seen at a great distance appear darker at the summit than at the base.') The *Trattato* was first published from scattered notes in French and Italian in 1651 but was well-known before that.

26. Le Plateau, Fonds régional d'art contemporain d'Île-de-France, opened 17 January, 2002. A space outside the perimeter of Paris-proper, it is an alternative to the 'alternative' space opened at Palais de Tokyo, in the heart of Paris (next to the Museum of

Modern Art of the City of Paris, Avenue de President Wilson, 16th arrondissement). Palais de Tokyo was opened in the same month as Le Plateau. Architect of le Plateau: Valode and Pistre/Jean-Marc Lalo. Cocktails at the grand opening of Le Plateau were provided by l'Espace Paul Ricard. BANG, a quarterly published by Editions Castermen and Beaux Arts magazine. Cocktails at launches also provided by Ricard SA.

27. *La Vierge et l'Enfant,* Ambrogio Lorenzetti. (1290–1348, Tuscany). This was the central panel of a polyptych, of which the other parts have not been identified. Remarkable for the healthy bite the Infant is taking from the fig in his hand, and for the natural beauty of the Virgin's face. Exhibited in its damaged state. This work was unknown to experts before it entered the collection of the Louvre in 1999. The Virgin's face is extraordinarily true-to-life. It contrasts with the stylised representation of the sacred in the remainder of the painting and with the faces of other Virgins in the vicinity.

28. *St George and the Dragon*, Paolo Uccello (1397–1475). Oil on canvas. 56.5 x 74cm. Painted c. 1460. National Gallery, London. Acquired from Lanckoronski Collection, Vienna, in 1959.

29. *Infant Jesus sending arrows of disease*, 1496. Title page from J. Grunpeck, *De Pestilentali Scorra, sive Mala de Franzos* (Augsburg, 1496).

30. *De Morbo Quem Gallicum Nuncupant*, Gilino, Coradino. Ferrara, 1497.

31. *The Physician*, Gerritt Dou (born and died in Leyden 1613–1675). Painted in 1653. Robert McDougall Gallery,

Christchurch, New Zealand until 2002. Now in the new Christchurch Art Gallery, Te Puna O Waiwhetu. Oil on copper. Bequeathed to city from the estate of Heathcote Helmore in 1965. Another version, oil on oak, exists in the Kunsthistorisches Museum, Vienna; this was exhibited in London between 16th April and 6th August, 2000. 49.3 x 37cm. The doctor in question is a *piskijker*, or urinomancer; in his hands a bowl of urine became a diagnostic tool. A snail appears at the bottom of the picture, an 'allusion to transience'; some flowers in a chipped bowl may, according to Ronnie Baer of the National Gallery of Art, Washington, refer to vanity. Anne-Claude-Philippe de Tubières, Comte de Caylus (1692–1765) read 'La Vie d'Antoine Watteau, peintre de figures et de paysages, sujets galants et modernes' to the Académie royale de peinture et de sculpture, le 3 fevrier 1748. E. & J. de Goncourt found the text at a *bouquiniste*. It was the first entry in their *L'Art du dix-huitième siècle,* published 1860 by A. Quantin, in Paris. This is how we know about Dou's fastidiousness: 'L'on cite entre autres sur ce point *Gérard Dow* et l'on remarque qu'il broïoit ses couleurs sur une glace, qu'il prenoit précautions infinies pour empêcher qu'elles fussent altérées par la moindre atôme de poussière et nettoïoit toujours lui-même sa palette et jusqu'a la hante de ses pinceaux, ce que le dernier auteur de la Vie des peintres a plaisamment entendu de son manche à balai, trompé par la double signification du mot hollandois qui suivant l'endroit et les circonstances où on l'emploie, signifie tantôt une hante de pinceau, tantôt un manche à balai, mais qui ne devoit pas faire d'équivoque ici.'

32. *The Young Mother.* Dou. 1655–66. Gemäldegalerie, Berlin. It is not the quality of Jules' slide which is at fault — even standing before the painting in the well-lit Gemäldegalerie, the urinomancer is hard to make out. Dou is known to have used a magnifying glass and to have worked very slowly towards the completion of his paintings.

33. *Young Woman with a Pearl Necklace.* 1662–65. Jan Vermeer (1632 Delft–1675 Delft). Until the end of the nineteenth century it was not uncommon for dealers to substitute the name of de Hooch for Vermeer's in order to effect a sale. Golden light enters the scene through leaded windows next to the wall-hung mirror. The vanishing point of the painting is just above the table so we are looking up at the woman, and cannot help admiring her as she admires herself, or the necklace. See Gérard de Lairesse, *Grosse Schilderboock 1*, 188–93 for the contemporary iconography of the pearl. Gemäldegalerie Berlin.

34. *The Sick Woman.* 1658–59. Gabriel Metsu (1629 Leyden–1667 Amsterdam). The only indication of material wealth is the woman's fur-hemmed jacket and her lace cap with its tear-drop glass or pearl weight. The weeping woman is also, presumably, wiping her eyes with her mistress's kerchief, also pendant-cornered. Very little is known of Metsu's life. A year before his marriage in Amsterdam in 1658, he had a notary public draw up a document announcing that he was now living in Amsterdam, and answering rumours which were making the rounds in Leyden, 'that he took a prostitute into the Academie and that he came out of a house of ill-repute in Leyden at six o'clock in the morning.'

(From Franklin W Robinson, *Gabriel Metsu (1629–1667)*). His paintings are more emotional than Dou's. He was 38 when he died.

35. *The Dropsical Woman* (*La Femme hydropique*) Wood panel. 86 x 67cm (with rounded top). Louvre. Gift of Charles-Emmanuel de Savoie in 1799 (the Louvre's first ever donated work).

36. *The Milkmaid*. (also known as *Milkmaid with Young Cowherd and Cow*). Lucas van Leyden (1489–1530, Leyden) 1510. 15.5 x 11.9cm. Rijksmuseum, Amsterdam.

37. *Woman with a Doe*. Lucas van Leyden. Signed with the monogram L and dated 1509. Engraving, 107 x 71mm. Acquired by The Hermitage, Saint Petersburg, from Yegor Makovsky in 1925. Early work. Lucas van Leyden is already concerned not with ideal form, but with creating an individualised human body. His Diana is represented in gentle communion with a long-limbed doe. In contrast with the *Diana* of the École de Fontainebleau, which possesses the ideal attributes of beauty admired by the French court (see Note 63), this Diana is bulky, highly muscled, and is evidently capable of incredible violence.

38. *The Toothache* (a.k.a. *The Pickpocket*, a.k.a. *The Charlatan*). Lucas van Leyden. 7.2 x 11.5cm.1523. Rijksmuseum, Amsterdam. Also Hermitage, St Petersburg. It shows a debt to German drawing in the grossness, awkwardness and materiality of its everyday characters.

39. *The Last Judgement*, Hieronymous Bosch (real name Jerome van Aken; c.1450–1516, Bois-le-duc). Oil on wood panel. Central panel (127 x 164cm), right wing (60 x 167cm), Akademie der Bildenden Künste, Vienna (another version is in Bruges). *The Hay-*

Wain. Right wing (45 x 135cm). Museo del Prado, Madrid. *The Garden of Earthly Delights.* Right wing (97 x 219cm), Museo del Prado, Madrid. *The Temptation of St Anthony*. Left wing (53 x 131cm). Museu Nacional de Arte, Antiga, Lisbon. None of his works are dated, but some can be ascribed to an early period and others such as the ones cited here to his mature period (*c*.1580 onwards). *Zwei Altarflügel,* Petrus Christus (1410–1472/73). 1452. Oak panels. Each of them 134 x 56 cm. Berliner Kulturforum.

40. 'To shave your head as Job did': Upon hearing that his sons and daughters had been killed by a falling building Job tore his clothes, shaved his head and lay with his face in the dust, saying, 'Naked I came from my mother's womb, and naked I will return there. The Lord gave and the Lord has taken, may the name of the Lord be blessed.' (Translation of Stephen Mitchell, *The Book of Job* (Kyle Cathie, London, 1989). Shaving the head in the manner of Job was prescribed by an Italian physician Ludovico Carri in 1498, as part of his treatment for the pox. The symptoms of the pox were similar to those described by Job when God permits Satan to blight Job's body: 'My innards boil and clamour; [...] My flesh blackens and peels; / all my bones are on fire. / And my harp is tuned to mourning, / my flute to the sound of tears.'

41. *Adoration of the dead Jesus Christ by Saint John the Evangelist and Mary Magdalene.* Attributed to Domenico of Paris (known from 1453 to 1492). Painted fired clay. 1.04 x 1.42M. Christ is flanked on the right by John, his hands clasped in prayer, and Mary Magdalene, who is holding His arm. In the Ferrarese style of the time. It could have been executed for the monastery of Santa

Maria delle Grazie, at Reggio nell' Emilia in 1470. Formerly in the collection of the Baron of Piqueras. Gift of Friends of the Louvre, 1971.

42. 'Description of a Struggle: The Supplicant's Story', Franz Kafka. First draft, unfinished, 1904–5. Text edition, Fischer, 1969. 'These Paris streets, they suddenly branch out, don't they? They are turbulent, aren't they? Things are not as they should be, how could they be, after all? (*Nicht wahr, diese Straßen von Paris sind plötzlich verzweigt; sie sind unruhig, nicht wahr? Es ist nicht alles in Ordnung, wie könnte es auch sein!*) Though we cannot be sure, these lines appear to have been written before Kafka visited Paris in 1911 with Max Brod, the man who refused to destroy Kafka's unpublished writings after his death (as Kafka had asked him to do), and who was responsible for bringing most of them to publication. Interestingly enough, there is no record of Edgar Allen Poe having visited Paris either. Poe (Boston, 1809–1849, Baltimore), in 'The Murders in the Rue Morgue', describes a Paris of private buildings and small streets which was largely demolished by Georges Eugène Haussman (1809–1891, prefect of the Seine *département* 1853–1870). Napoleon III encouraged Haussman, who raised public loans to demolish private building and cut wide boulevards through the labyrinthine lanes. Poe crossed the Atlantic (from Norfolk, Virginia to Liverpool) as a child and spent five years at school in Britain (1815–1820). His descriptions of France are probably based on information received from travellers and from literature itself. It is after having left their 'time-eaten and grotesque mansion' in a 'retired and desolate portion of the

Faubourg St Germain', while strolling at night down 'a long dirty street, in the vicinity of the Palais Royal' that Monsieur C. Auguste Dupin explains how he knew what his companion, the author of the story, had been thinking during the preceding fifteen minutes! 'The Murders in the Rue Morgue' is regarded as the first detective story. (Published in *Graham's Magazine*, of which he was editor, in 1841).

43. Apuleius, Lucius. Alive 2nd century A.D. Born at Madauros, in Numidia (near the modern Mdaourouch in Algeria) in A.D.125. So, like Mélita, he was, in a sense, a *pied-noir*. Educated at Carthage and Athens. Author of *Metamorphoses* or *The Golden Ass*, story of a man accidentally turned into an ass. The earliest Latin novel, it describes, among other things, an organised criminal gang and urban occult practices. An expert rhetorician, he successfully defended himself against charges of sorcery before the African proconsul Claudius Maximus. Thereafter, he devoted himself to literature and philosophy.

44. Squarepusher is a drummer, bassist, guitarist and keyboardist in one, both individual and group. The disk *Music is Rotten One Note* was released by Sheffield's Warp label in 1999.

45. *Confessions*. Aurelius Augustinus (Tagaste (the modern Souk-Ahras), 355–430, Hippo Regius (the modern Bône on the Algerian coast). Espoused then rejected the Manichaean system of belief before being converted to his mother's religion. His conversion occurred after he opened a volume of St Paul at random and read: 'No further would I read, nor needed I; for instantly at the end of this sentence, by a light as it were of a serenity infused into my

heart, all the darkness of doubt vanished away.' A close friend died when he was a student. *Verus philosophus est amator Dei* ('The true philosopher is the lover of God'). *De civitate Dei* (viii, 1).

46. *The Parthenon.* Masterminded by Pericles, completed under the supervision of Phidias, dedicated to Athena 439BC, dedicated to Virgin Mary 450AD, turned into a Catholic church 1204, into a mosque 1458, and bombed by Venetians 1687. 253 of its sculptures were granted to Thomas Bruce (Earl of Elgin) by the occupying Turks. Earl Elgin removed them from Athens at great personal expense in 1801–3. Sold cheaply to the British Government in 1816 to establish quasi-legality, they were later installed in the British Museum. Greece wants them back. Byron called them 'plunder from a bleeding land'.

47. Jules at the National Gallery 1956: Titian, *An Allegory of Prudence* 1565–70. Presented by David Koetser in 1966. Inscribed EX PRAETERITO PRAESENS PRUDENTER AGIT NI FUTUR– ACTIONE DETURPET (From the past the man of the present acts prudently so as not to imperil the future). The left head resembles Titian himself in old age. The triple-headed beast (wolf, lion and do) was a symbol of prudence. Oil on canvas 76.2 x 68.6 cm. El Greco, *The Agony in the Garden of Gethsemane*. Late 16th century. Oil on Canvas. 102 x 131 cm. Acquired 1919. El Greco suffered from irregular curvature of the cornea, which would have prevented light rays from converging as they should on his retina. Some say this explains his particular way of representing the light. *The Bathers*, (*Les Grandes Baigneuses*), Paul Cézanne. Painted 1900–1906, acquired 1964. 127.2 x 196.1cm.

48. The great rose windows of Notre Dame were completed circa 1220 (west), 1250–55 (north) and 1260 (south). Jules is looking at the one in the south arm of the transept. Christ on a throne is encircled by apostles and martyrs. A line of prophets below was added in the nineteenth century under the supervision of Viollet-le-Duc, who was also responsible for rotating the great rose (presumably for structural reasons), thus making a rib lie at 12 o-clock and not an arced window.

49. *Ship of Fools* (*La Nef des Fous*), Hieronymous Bosch (c.1450–1516, Bois-le-duc). Wood panel. 58 x 32 cm. Gift of Camille Benoit, former conservateur of The Louvre, in 1918. The ship allegory featured in popular customs associated with the days preceding Ash Wednesday. In 1494 Sebastian Brant published *Das Narrenschiff* (*navis stultifera, Ship of Fools*), a satirical verse allegory with 112 separate woodcuts (some by Albrecht Dürer) using as its framework the voyage of a ship of fools setting sail for Narragonia (Idiotland). The fool figures in western literature from the antisocial provocation of the Cynics to Dostoevski's idiot prince without a clear line of cause and effect, but it is certain that Brant's work influenced Desiderius Erasmus' *The Praise of Folly* and the good-humoured moralising of Hans Sachs. 'It is safe to assume that these woodcuts inspired the iconography of the entire range of polemical illustrations of the era of the Lutheran Reformation, at least in so far as they established and fixed symbols that were readily assimilable by everybody: the fool motif runs through the whole period in many permutations of purpose.' (H. Robinson Hammerstein, 'Word and Image in Early Modern German Print',

Trinity College Dublin, 1986) The first occupant of Brant's ship is the 'Book Fool', who cherishes and protects books which 'he neither reads carefully nor understands'.

50. *Tombeau de Philippe Pot de Citeaux*, attributed to Pierre Antoine le Moiturier (Avignon, c.1425–c.1500). Carved c.1477–83. Philippe Pot was Lord High Steward and in 1477 (year of the commission), Grand Seneschal (High Bailiff) of Burgundy. He died in 1494. The sculpture was transferred from the Abbey of Citeaux to The Louvre in 1889. The mourners are not identified, their facial characteristics are obscured, but each carries a different heraldic shield.

51. 'Out avisedness' ('without thought') occurs in 'A Lover's Confession' by Charles of Orléans (1394–1465). It seems to be the song of a woman telling her father of her stolen kiss.

52. Museum of Cluny. Once the Paris residence of the Benedictine Cluny monks (based in a huge monastery in the valley of the Grosne near Lyon). Its construction combined elements of gothic architecture and renaissance styles. It was built between 1485 and 1500 near the Roman thermal baths (2nd century), and became the property of the state in 1790 (in the years that followed 1789 the monastery to the south was largely destroyed). It now houses several priceless collections and is the site of temporary touring exhibitions.

53. Antonio Pollaiuolo (Florence, 1431–Rome 1498). *Martyrdom of Saint Sebastian* (1475), originally in the Chapel of the Pucci at St Sebastiona of the Servites. It is a portrait of Gino di Ludovico Capponi. Antonio 'dissected many bodies to examine their anato-

my' (Vasari). The portrait is now in the National Gallery, London.

54. *The Beggar's Opera,* Thomas Gay (1685–1732):
> *Tis woman that seduces all mankind,*
> *By her we first were taught the wheedling arts.*

55. *Letter Rack.* Hoogstraaten, Samuel van (1627– 1678, Dordrecht). Like Dou, he was a student of Rembrandt, and, like Vermeer, he studied under Fabritius, who experimented with convex mirror painting. A very well connected artist, most of his later works included a medallion presented by the Hapsburg Emperor Ferdinand III. The medallion commemorated the fact that he had fooled the emperor into mistaking a section of one of his works for the reality it represented. Later in life Hoogstraaten developed a following for his perspective effects and did not stop short of producing a series of immensely popular peepshow boxes (there is one in the National Gallery, London), that gave the viewer an illusion of three-dimensional reality. He believed a good painter should 'not only concern himself with the dead body of art and follow the trend of the day and do as others do, but he should be infatuated with the soul of art: that is to say he should seek to investigate the actual qualities of nature. He should be jealous when someone else knows something which is unknown to him, and ashamed to learn something from someone else indirectly, seeking rather to figure it out by his own effort.' Book I, Chapter 1, *Introduction to the Academy of Painting; or, The Visible World* (Rotterdam, 1678), translated by Hester Ysseling for *Art in Theory, 1648–1815,* published in the UK and USA in 2000. Views such as the following were held by many Dutch artists at the time: 'The

determinations of a thing consist of length, breadth, height and depth, concavity and roundness, straightness and curvature, bias and obliqueness, and in such a variety of ways as can be drawn from lines and points to make out any kind of shape. It is by means of lines, then, that we should learn to reproduce things in nature as they appear to us. This is where the art of perspective comes into play, because the eye does not comprehend things in their entirety but only the faces which are turned towards us. What the eye sees ends at the boundary set by the outline, which is made by the limits [*zichteynden*] of the rays which are cast by our eyes.' (*ibid* Book I, Chapter 7).

56. *Les Bourgeois de Calais*, August Rodin (Paris, 1840–Meudon, 1917). Bronze, 1884–1886. Museum of Art, Philadelphia, 210 x 140 x 190cm. (Also Rodin Museum, Paris). In honour of the citizens who offered their lives to save Calais from destruction ('stone by stone') and the massacre of its population ('one by one') during occupation by the forces of Edward III of England in 1347. The completion of a work on this theme was also a triumph over something of a jinx! David d'Angers made a rough model (*maquette*) on the subject (different in form from Rodin's finished bronzes), but the work was abandoned due to lack of funds. Two of his pupils knew the same failure; the sculptor Baptiste Clésinger had been about to start work on it when the war of 1870 broke out.

57. *Le Tour de Travail* (*Tower of Work*), Rodin. Not completed. Plaster model at Rodin museum, Paris; larger model at Meudon. Rodin wrote of a dozen or so turns of a spiral (perhaps 35 metres high on a base of 8m2), but the model has only seven turns. Text

written on the base of the draft: 'Projet d'un Monument au Travail. Dans la crypte: les mineurs, les scaphandriers. Autour de la porte: le Jour et la Nuit. Et autour de la colonne, les métiers: les maçons, charpentiers, forgerons, menuisiers, potiers etc. en costume de l'époque. En haut: Les Bénédictions viennent du ciel. On a essayé de rappeler la ruche, le phare.' This unfinished tower neglects the oldest profession in the world, unlike the tomb of Alyattes, described by Herodotus as having a circumference of three quarters of a mile and a breadth of four hundred yards. On that monument, recently excavated by archaeologists, was inscribed the proportionate amount of work done by its builders, a collection of tradesmen, craftsmen *and prostitutes*. The prostitutes had done the most work. Herodotus describes another tomb, the pyramid of Cheops, inscribed with the amount spent on radishes, onions, and leeks for the slave-labourers during the ten years it took to build it. It is not known whether Rodin was aware of these tombs. In his notes he only mentions as influences the Trajan Column in Rome (dedicated 113 A.D.), 'Tours des Vents' (wind-towers with an Italian flavour popular in 19th century French and German landscaping), and the highly significant Trajan-like column in the Place Vendôme (see Note 8 about Courbet, who was arraigned for having ordered its demolition).

58. *Gospel According to Luke*, xiii, 4. The Tower of Siloe was probably part of the Jerusalem city wall. According to John, ix, 1–7, Christ gave sight to a man born blind at the pool of Siloe, just outside the south wall. The pool gave its name to the whole vicinity. Isaiah (viii,6) compares the House of David to 'the waters of Siloe,

that go in silence.'

59. *Pupils stoning their teacher by order of Camillus.* Nicolas Poussin (Villers, 1594–1665, Rome). Louvre. A teacher, unnamed, took his pupils out of a besieged city and offered them to the siege-laying Roman general as hostages. The general, Camillus, was outraged at the suggestion. He ordered his lictors to strip off the teacher's clothing and tie his hands. According to Plutarch, he then furnished the boys with rods and ordered them to scourge him, 'to punish the traitor, and whip him into the city.' Poussin has the pupils stone him. The humiliated wrist-tied teacher tries in vain to escape the loaded fists of his students. Camillus' left hand is stretched out, commanding. The hands of soldiers clutch upright standard staffs, symbols no longer of power, but of correct behaviour in time of war. At the top of the central, most ornate of those standards, is an open palm, deathly, pallid. In reality, (as it is recorded by Plutarch), Camillus returned the boys to the Falerii, who subsequently opened their gates to the Romans saying that Camillus was an honourable man. A truce was agreed upon. The poorly paid soldiers, however, who had been hoping for plenty of booty, were disappointed. They denounced Camillus, who was later exiled. (Plutarch's *Lives*, Camillus viii 5 x i). The painting was completed in 1637 for Louis Phélypeaulx de la Vrillière. (Félibien). 252 x 268cm. It decorated Vrillière's Parisian 'hôtel' which became that of the Count of Toulouse then that of the Duke of Penthièvre. It was confiscated in 1794.

60. Phidias, designer and to some extent sculptor of the Parthenon (see below), was accused by enemies of pilfering gold

designated for his statues and of introducing his own effigy into his work, which was strictly forbidden. (If he did in fact represent himself, it was as a bald old man taking up a stone with both hands.)

61. The Woman with a Doe exhibits symptoms of childhood Porphyria, a metabolic illness that is transferred genetically. In children the skin can be so sensitive to light that it blisters horribly. It turns the teeth and bones reddish brown, like the soil around volcanoes. It was once believed to have been caused by vampires. (See Winkler, Mary G. and Karl E. Anderson, 'Vampires, Porphyria and the Media: medicalisation of a myth'. *Perspectives on Biology and Medicine* 33: 598–611).

62. *The Lady and the Unicorn*, by an unknown artist. 3.77 x 4.73M. 1480+. Possibly commissioned by Jean Le Viste of Lyons, circa 1489. Tapestry. Paris (cartoons), Flanders (woven). Wool and silk. Certainly completed by 1500. Noticed by Prosper Mérimée at the Chateau de Boussac (Creuse) in 1841. George Sand wrote about it several times, increasing interest. Some lower areas had been destroyed by damp and imperfectly replaced. It was acquired by the Cluny Museum, Paris, in 1882 and is now exhibited with a maximum light strength of 50 lux, to preserves the fabric. The work is made up of six tapestries : Mon Seul Désir (renunciation), Smell, Hearing, Touch, Taste, and Sight. This last one, (La Vue), is Jules' favourite.

63. *Diana the Huntress*. School of Fontainebleau, circa 1550. Canvas, 1.91 x 1.32. Acquired in 1840 by the Louvre for 226 francs from the sale of the Lebreton estate (Gilles Lebreton was the mas-

ter mason commissioned to build Fontainebleau for François 1er in 1528). A copy was then commissioned for 400 francs. This Diana couldn't be more different than Lucas van Leyden's earlier Diana, the Woman with a Doe. The personage of Diana became popular in poetry and painting during the time of Henry II because it permitted an allusion to Diane de Poitiers, duchess of Valentinois and mistress of Henry II, and because of the passion of French kings for hunting.

64. *Legal Code of Hammurabi*, anonymous. 225 x 55cm. Unearthed 1901–2 by the French Delegation to Persia at Susa (once the capital of Elam and, later, of Persia). Carved 1792–1750BC. Louvre. It is a black diorite obelisk-like stele containing carved images and 39 columns of wedge-written laws in exemplary sentences such as the one about punishment for inept eye surgeons. Hammurabi was Babylon's sixth king.

65. *The Judas Kiss*. Hans Holbein the elder (Augsburg, 1460 or 1465–1524, Isenheim). Wood, 88 x86 cm. Completed around the end of the 1490s. It is held in the private collection of Prince von Fürstenberg at Donaueschingen, in the heart of the Schwarzwald (Black Forest). *The Judas Kiss* opposes characteristics supposedly divine and profane. His highly-praised portraits combined the two. It is believed he made a trip to the Netherlands around 1490. Experts speak about the influence of Rogier van der Weyden. He knew professional success but was forced to leave his native Augsburg because of his debts. Having learned something about portraiture from his father, Hans Holbein the Younger (Augsburg, 1497?–London, 1543) completed many portraits in England. He

benefited from the outlawing of religious painting there, completing, at the end of his life, a string of secular portraits for Henry VIII. The great flourishing of portrait painting during the reign of the Stuarts in England was to follow.

66. *Il n'y a pas d'amour heureux*, Louis Aragon (Paris, 1897–1982). 'Mon bel amour, mon cher amour / Ma déchirure / Je te porte dans moi / Comme un oiseau blessé...', (My love, my dear love, my wound, I carry you within like an injured bird, and those ones, without knowing, watch us go by, repeating after me these words I have braided, words which, for your great eyes, immediately died. Love knows no contentment.) Il n'y a pas d'amour heureux [Literally, 'There is no (such thing as) happy love'] — Louis Aragon's poem was set to music by Georges Brassens and sung by many artists in the latter part of the twentieth century. Used with grateful acknowledgement.

A precursor of Alpha Books published a limited edition (in 1983 in Christchurch, New Zealand) of a translation by Carol S. Woodward of Aragon's *Système DD* (from *Les Aventures de Télémaque*, Gallimard, 1922). A full-page reproduction of its unusual jacket (red and black screenprint on brown corrugated cardboard by multi-media artist Stuart Page) can be found on page 94 of *Album Aragon* ('Iconographie choisie et commentée par Jean Ristat'), Éditions Gallimard, 1997.

67. *Calypso's cave*. Jan Bruegel the Elder (Brussels, 1568–1625, Antwerp). Johnny van Haeften Gallery, London.

68. Jacques Lacan, 'The Field of the Other and Back to the Transference' in *The Four Fundamental Concepts of Psycho-analysis*.

First published Éditions du Seuil, 1973.

69. *Ecce Homo*, by the School of Bartholemew Bruyn the Elder, or Bruyn himself (c. 1493 Niederrhein–1555 Cologne). Oak panel, 184 x 84cm. 1525. Wallraf-Richartz-Museum, Cologne. The scene is from the passion of Christ. See Ruth Mellinkoff, *Outcasts: Signs of Otherness in Northern European Art of the Late Middle Ages* (University of California Press, 1993). Mellinkoff notes also (p.188) that in the art of this period shaved heads signify criminals, slaves or serfs. The medieval origins of the 'fingers' sign is noted in the *figo* (V-horned gesture) and other vulgar signs such as the *mano fica* (thumb between 1st and 2nd fingers, hand fisted) etc.

70. 'Les Lettres de rémission accordées à François Villon' in *Villon Hier et aujourd'hui*, Jean Derens, Jean Dufournet and Michael Freeman (eds). Bibliothèque historique de la Ville de Paris, Paris, 1993. pp.53–67.

71. Fernand Léger (Argentan, 1881–1955, Gif-sur-Yvette). Trained first as an architect. During World War he met men from many walks of life, men he would not otherwise have come to know. He and many of his new companions suffered the destructive effects of gas poisoning. Thereafter he attempted to create art that would be accessible to all, especially working men. He sought poetry in the delineation of everyday or industrial objects.

72. *De l'Esprit des Lois*. Montesquieu, Charles le Secondat (Bordelais, 1689–1755, Paris). *Nous ne voyons point, dans les histoires, que les Romains se fissent mourir sans sujet : mais les Anglais se tuent, sans qu'on puisse imaginer aucune raison qui les y détermine ; ils se tuent dans le sein même du bonheur. Cette action, chez les Romains, était l'effet de l'édu-*

cation ; elle tenait à leur manière de penser et à leurs coutumes : chez les Anglais elle est l'effet d'une maladie ; elle tient à l'état physique de la machine, et est indépendante de toute autre cause. [...] Il est clair que les lois civiles de quelques pays ont eu des raisons pour flétrir l'homicide de soi-même : mais, en Angleterre, on ne peut pas plus le punir qu'on ne punit les effets de la démence. ('We see nothing, in history, to suggest that the Romans committed suicide without good reason: but the English kill themselves without our being able to imagine any reason that has made them take that resolve ; they kill themselves in the midst of good fortune. This action, among the Romans, was the result of education; it was contiguous to their manner of thinking and to their customs: among the English it is the result of an illness; it is related to the state of the bodily apparatus, and is independent of all other cause. [...] It is clear that the civil laws of some countries have had their reasons pour condemning self-murder: but, in England, one can not condemn it any more than one can condemn the effects of dementia.'). Livre XIV, ch. xii.

73. Jean Dubuffet (1901–1985). Several of his chunky statues can be found in public and private places in Paris. Paint or polyurethane on epoxy resin. Dubuffet championed the theory of Art Brut ('raw art'), asserting the validity of graffiti, of the work of the mentally ill, or of persons wholly untrained (in the conventional sense).

74. *Waterloo Sunset* (Ray Davies) is perhaps the most popular song recorded by The Kinks.

75. Fra Filippo Lippi died of quinsy at forty five. Domenico Ghirlandaio of fever at forty four. Antonio da Correggio from

drinking dubious well-water at forty.

76. *Fragments,* Menander (in Greek Menandros) (c.342–c.292, Athens).'The man who stays too long dies disgusted; his old age is painful and tedious; he is poor and in need. Whichever way he turns he sees enemies; people conspire against him. He did not go when he should have gone; he has not died a good death.'

77. Gorky, Archile (Vosdanig Manoog Adoian) (1904–48). Stands at the intersection where European Surrealism merged into the current of American Abstract Expressionism. Fire destroyed his recent works the same year he was operated on for cancer. He broke his neck in a car accident, his wife left him, he hanged himself.

78. Elsheimer, Adam (1578–1610). An immensely popular German artist who worked in Italy mainly on copper. Highly sensitive to light and landscape, and the placement of figures therein. He was, however, personally unsuccessful, subject to depression, and died in poverty. Greatly admired by Rembrandt, who arraigned him after his death for not having worked hard enough. De Witte, Emanuel (1617–1692), a contemporary of de Hooch, suffered grave social alienation and debt. His daughter was arraigned for theft and his wife deported for having encouraged her.

79. *The Martyrdom of St Erasmus,* Poussin. Completed 1628–1629. Città del Vaticano, Rome. Poussin settled in Rome in 1624 and lived there for the rest of his long life, excepting an unhappy return to Paris 1640-2. He married the daughter of French cook Jacques Dughet, who was working in Rome. Regarding the practice of drawing intestines from live victims, see the sacrifice of a

bristly boar and an unshorn sheep of two years old in The Aeneid, Book 12, ll 213–215. Saint Erasmus was martyred during the reign of Diocletian c. 303 AD.

80. The Wallace fountains were offered to the city of Paris by English philanthropist Richard Wallace (London, 1818–Paris, 1890) whose widow, in 1897, bequeathed the art collection of Hertford House, Manchester Square, London. The fountains feature three goddesses. Each used to have a goblet on a chain for taking a drink of the spring water. These were discontinued, for reasons of public health, in 1952.

81. 'The Fisherman and his Soul,' Oscar Wilde (Dublin, 1854–1900, Paris). First published in *A House of Pomegranates* in 1891, the same year as *The Picture of Dorian Gray*. Wilde died bankrupt. His body was buried in a pauper's grave. Later, friends arranged for its reinterment in Père Lachaise cemetery.

82. The bust of the critic Castagnary can be found in semi-darkness under the road bridge that crosses Montmartre Cemetery. That cemetery itself is a kind of concealment. It was dedicated after the near-revolution of 1871, not least because an enormous number of citizens had died on the site. It is said also that the cathedral of Sacré Coeur, on the summit of Montmartre, was built on blood.

83. *First Epistle to the Corinthians*. Paul the Apostle. '…when that which is perfect is come, then that which is in part shall be done away. When I was a child, I spake as a child, I understood as a child, I thought as a child: but when I became a man, I put away childish things. For now we see through a glass, darkly; but then

face to face: now I know in part; but then shall I know even as also I am known.' 13 x–xii (King James Version)

84. *Virgin flanked by male and female religious personages*, attributed to the atelier of Daniel Mauch (Ulm 1477–Liege, 1540). Linden wood, then coloured c.1505. The centre-piece Virgin is lost. Beneath the folds of her ample robe sheltered, on one side, a hierarchy of ecclesiastical males, including two popes; this is in the Donatello Room of the Louvre (donated by Elizabeth Mège, 1958). Its counterpart, a covey of religious women is housed in the Tiroler Landesmuseum Ferdinandeum, Innsbruck.

85. Dreyfus, Alfred (1859–1935). French captain during the third republic. Falsely accused of treason, he was defended by intellectuals such as Émile Zola who, in publishing 'J'Accuse' on January 13, 1898 on the front page of *Aurore*, established a tradition of intellectuals speaking out against right wing tendencies, racism, fraud and misuses of power. This tradition would culminate in the formulations of Jean-Paul Sartre and Guy Debord and the student-workers revolt in Paris, 1968. More recently it has been seen at work in varied ways, such as the pro-Palestinian stance of Jean Genet (1910–1986) and the writings of, among others, sociologist Pierre Bourdieu (1930–2002). The statue was a state commission finished by Tim in 1985. It was to stand in the École Militaire, site of Dreyfus's degradation, but the army refused to give its consent. So it was placed in the Jardin des Tuileries for a while and was finally given a neglected triangle, Place Pierre Lafue, on boulevard Raspail, not far from Jules' flat. The bronze sculpture is characterised by enormous feet and hands, a broken sword, heavy clothing

with the suggestion of a frail figure underneath. In December 1999 the City of Paris named a square in the 15th arrondissement after the ill-treated captain. On February 1st, 2002, when I visited the statue for details, it had been vandalised with fluorescent-yellow spray paint, and the words 'Sale traître' ('Dirty traitor') had really been daubed upon its base.

86. *Odes.* Horace (born Quintus Horatius Flaccus) (Venusia, 65–8BC, Rome).

> *Why for lands that an alien sun*
> *Warms exchange our own? Has an exile ever*
> *Fled from himself too?*

(Book 2 xvi lines 8-20. From *Odes & Carmen Saeculare.* Translated in the original metre by Guy Lee. Frances Cairns, 1999).

87. *The Annunciation.* Simone di Martino (Sienna. c.1283–1344, Avignon). 1333. Palazzo degli Uffizi, Florence. Originally in the chapel of the Sienna cathedral. In four pointed arches are medallion figures of the prophets Jeremiah, Ezechiel, Isaiah and Daniel. The figures of St Ansan and St Margaret to the left and right of the annunciation scene are by Lippo Memmi from designs by Simone, his brother-in-law. Distemper on wood. 2.65 x 3.05M. A life-giving breath circulates around the kneeling angel, as words written in gold pass from her before some unopened lily flowers to the modest virgin, who, in her manner, conceives the message.

88. *Hommage à Apollinaire*, Pablo Picasso (Ruiz Y Picasso) (Malaga, 1881–1973, Mougins). Unsigned, bronze. The work is a portrait of Picasso's partner from 1936 till 1944, Dora Maar. It

went missing from a tiny park opposite rue Guillaume Apollinaire in St Germain des Prés, Paris, in March 1999. It was discovered but not recognized a few weeks after its theft, in the moat of the park of the Castle of Osny, Val d'Oise (50 km from Paris). Since the police failed to identify it as a stolen work, the mayoralty put it on display in the reception area of the adjacent town hall. The town council announced its discovery to the Direction Régionale des Affaires Culturelles, who, in turn, notified the police section concerned with the traffic of cultural objects. No one made any connection with the theft in Paris. The bust was not identified for nearly two years, and then by a local inhabitant. It is now in its former home, Square Laurent Prache, shaded by the ancient abbey. Both Apollinaire and Picasso had been questioned by police earlier in the century regarding the theft of another work eventually returned to its former home, the *Mona Lisa*.

89. 'L'art est visible, comme Dieu.' and 'L'art est un produit pharmaceutique pour imbéciles' are part of a Dada manifesto published in the journal *391*, March 1920 (held at Bibliothèque Paul Destribats, Paris) by Francis Picabia (1878–1953, Paris). It was dedicated to poem-drawings and other graphic work. There were nineteen issues between 1917 and 1924. The Eight was the name of a group of American painters who exhibited together in 1908 with the aim of bringing painting back in touch with real life.

90. Bartimaeus (son of Timaeus) called to Jesus from the roadside and would not let up when told to be quiet by those around about. Christ restored his sight saying, 'thy faith hath made thee whole' (*Mark,* x, 46-52) or 'thy faith hath saved thee' (*Luke,* xviii,

35-43) (King James Version).
91. *Revelations,* xxi,1.

PRINTED AND BOUND BY ASTRA PRINT
WELLINGTON, NEW ZEALAND
SEPTEMBER 2003